MW01133595

Cheyenne Warrior II

Hawk

Two Screenplays

by

Michael B. Druxman

Copyright © 2003 The Pacific Trust

Copyright © 2012 Michael B. Druxman

All rights reserved.

ISBN-13:
978-1468181692

ISBN-10:
1468181696

In Memory of
My high school Drama teacher,
Mrs. Patricia Borgstrom,
who believed.

CONTENTS

ACKNOWLEDGMENTS

My thanks to the many worldwide fans of *Cheyenne Warrior*, particularly Linda Moore, whose letters, phone calls and encouragement have helped to keep the story of "Soars Like a Hawk" alive for almost twenty years.

INTRODUCTION

Cheyenne Warrior (1994) was produced by Roger Corman's Concorde/New Horizons Pictures, under the direction of Mark Griffiths. The picture starred Kelly Preston, Dan Haggerty, Bo Hopkins and Pato Hoffmann.

The movie was a critical and financial success, and through home video and cable television, achieved a worldwide fan following that persists to the present day. So popular was the picture that, in 1998, The Center Press published a paperback edition of my original screenplay.

I've written extensively about the genesis, production history and success of *Cheyenne Warrior* in both that paperback and in my 2010 memoir, *My Forty-Five Years in Hollywood...And How I Escaped Alive*, hence I am not going to repeat that chronicle here.

Some of the fans that wrote to me wanted to know if there would be a sequel to *Cheyenne Warrior*. I had never considered doing a follow-up to my original story, but once the suggestion was made, I started thinking in that direction.

The problem was that, having sold my screenplay to Roger Corman, he now owned the characters, as well as any sequel rights, and he was hesitant to commit to a second film. Westerns were, and still are, a difficult sell in the marketplace, particularly when the central character is a woman.

Face it. There is no female John Wayne, Gary Cooper or Clint Eastwood.

Nevertheless, when I wasn't working on another writing project, I started developing a follow-up to *Cheyenne Warrior*; one that would reunite the characters of Rebecca (played by Kelly Preston) and Soars Like a Hawk (Pato Hoffmann).

A few years passed and I, ultimately, came up with a storyline that I really liked, but Roger was still not willing to move forward with a sequel. So, I decided to write this new story anyway. I would change the names of the characters and make some cursory adjustments to the plot, but the primary theme, emotional elements and other aspects of the story I had developed would remain the same.

The finished script is called *Sarah Golden Hair*, and I think it is one the best screenplays I have ever written. Unfortunately, it is a Western and, as of this writing, remains unproduced. However, if you would like to read it, it is available in both paperback and Kindle editions.

About a year after I completed *Sarah Golden Hair*, Roger hired me to write a sequel to *Cheyenne Warrior*.

Since I had used my previously developed plot for *Sarah Golden Hair*, I now had to come up with a new narrative and this one, as it turned out, eliminated altogether the character of Rebecca. *Cheyenne Warrior II* would focus on Soars Like a Hawk and, except for it being a Western about Native Americans, the only thing that it really has in common with *Sarah Golden Hair* is that both stories begin with the infamous Sand Creek Massacre of November 29, 1864, in which a group of Colorado Militia slaughtered over one hundred peaceful Cheyenne men, women and children.

I completed the first draft of *Cheyenne Warrior II* and, frankly, I was quite happy with it. Aside from the fact that it was a good script, I felt that its conclusion could generate a second sequel, which would complete a trilogy, and/or the screenplay could serve as a backdoor pilot for a television series featuring the character of Hawk.

Sadly, Roger and his staff did not agree.

There was no problem with my writing, but they thought that the story lacked the romantic element, which had made the original *Cheyenne Warrior* so popular, particularly with women viewers. In other words, they wanted me to do a major rewrite and, following some contract renegotiations, I agreed.

From a basic story standpoint, *Hawk*, the second version of the sequel, is pretty much the same as the first. The major difference is the addition of the "Rose Carmichael" character, who dominates much of the action.

I don't want to be a spoiler, so before I comment further on either script, I'm going to let you read them, then I will share my thoughts and relate the rest of the "behind the scenes" proceedings in the "Afterword".

Please keep in mind when you read these scripts that these are, essentially, revised first draft screenplays. They would serve as an initial roadmap for directors and actors when the movie goes into production.

Scenes would be revised; dialogue would be rewritten and some lines would even be dropped, since a good actor can often convey a writer's emotional intent without saying a word.

Since there are no actors here to perform this book, the only way for me to communicate my intent to you, the reader, is to leave my original, sometimes perhaps a bit wordy, dialogue intact.

On the other hand, feel free to stand in front of a mirror and convey my emotional intent aloud.

One final suggestion: After you finish reading *Cheyenne Warrior II*, wait a few days before you read *Hawk*. That way, you will approach the second script with a refreshed viewpoint and, hopefully, will avoid skipping over sequences that appear familiar.

Michael B. Druxman

"CHEYENNE WARRIOR II"

EXT. MOUNTAIN TRAIL. DAY.

A wooded mountain trail, somewhere in the Rocky Mountains.
Patches of snow are on the ground.

UNDER THE CREDITS, we watch a band of four Cheyenne braves,
a hunting party, make their way on horseback along the ridge. They
have two pack horses, one of which has a dead elk strapped across
its back.

Leader of the group, riding a pinto, is SOARS LIKE A HAWK
(30s), a handsome gallant warrior with strong, classic features. A
charismatic, level-headed leader, Hawk is in line to become a
Council chief. He carries a Henry rifle.

Others in the group include TALL ELK (30s), a pragmatic warrior
with a stately bearing, CRAZY BUFFALO (late 20s), tall, muscular
and sullen, and YELLOW MOCCASIN (30s), who listens more than
he talks. They are armed with bow and arrows and older, single shot
rifles.

As CREDITS END, a nearby GUNSHOT is heard. The Cheyenne
exchange glances, then Crazy Buffalo gallops ahead to investigate.
Hawk kicks his horse; hurries after him, while the other two
Cheyenne follow more slowly.

Several hundred yards ahead of the others, Crazy Buffalo reins his
horse, dismounts; looks down into the valley.

CRAZY BUFFALO'S P.O.V.

About a half mile away, a WHITE TRAPPER holds up the rabbit he
has shot with his rifle. He is unaware of the nearby Cheyenne.

BACK TO SCENE

Hawk arrives; reins his horse; dismounts, just as Crazy Buffalo raises his rifle, gets ready to shoot the trapper.

[NOTE: Dialogue within quotation marks is spoken in the appropriate Native American language, with English subtitles.]

                    CRAZY BUFFALO
          "He is hunting on Cheyenne land."

                         HAWK
          "If you kill that white man, the soldiers will come. They
          will attack our people."
                        (*Beat*)
          "Crazy Buffalo, my future brother-in-law, it is only a
          rabbit."

                    CRAZY BUFFALO
          "It is a Cheyenne rabbit."

Tall Elk and Yellow Moccasin have arrived on the scene with the pack horses.

                         HAWK
          "The Pawnee come on our land. Maybe their rabbits come
          here, too."

                    CRAZY BUFFALO
          "Soars Like A Hawk talks like his white friends. He sounds
          like a woman."

                         HAWK
                     (*Ignoring him*)
          "No, I think that is a Pawnee rabbit. The white man will eat
          it and get a belly ache."

As Tall Elk and Yellow Moccasin chuckle at Hawk's joke, he remounts his horse.

Seeing that his companions will not back him up, Crazy Buffalo begrudgingly lowers his rifle; remounts his horse.

The Cheyenne continue on their way.

EXT. CHEYENNE CAMP. DAY.

A Cheyenne winter camp. Patches of snow are on the ground. Dozens of teepees are clustered together at a horseshoe bend of the shallow creek. Horses are tethered away from the teepees.

Cheyenne men, women and children peacefully go about their daily chores. Among them are WHITE ANTELOPE (40), one of the chiefs, RUNNING WOLF (17), a young brave, eager to prove himself, who is working on his bow, and LITTLE BUTTERFLY (18), an attractive Cheyenne maiden, soon to be Hawk's bride. She is carrying a jug of water toward one of the teepees.

TITLE CARD: "Sand Creek, Colorado Territory, November 29, 1864."

White Antelope, who has been talking with a Cheyenne Brave, glances off, and sees:

WHITE ANTELOPE'S P.O.V.

A troop of several hundred Militia, both in uniform and civilian clothing, are taking their positions along the ridge of the hill above the camp. Cannons are being made ready to fire.

BACK TO SCENE

All of the Cheyenne appear anxious, confused.

Little Butterfly gasps in fear; drops her jug. It smashes onto the ground.

Women and children run to their teepees.

ATOP THE RIDGE

The Militia continues its preparations for the attack.

Leader of the force is COLONEL JOHN M. CHIVINGTON (43), tall, burly, bearded; dressed in full uniform. A Methodist minister, he has been described as "a crazy preacher who thinks he's Napoleon Bonaparte".

Surrounding him are three scruffy opportunistic drifters in civilian clothes, none of whom you would ever invite to your home for dinner. They are JAMES COCHRAN (late 30s), an Irish immigrant/buffalo hunter, BILLY RAY BEDFORD (30s), a Confederate Army deserter from Alabama and BRIAN PUGH (20s), a young man with a slight build and the mentality of a child, who does Cochran's every bidding.

Also among the Militia is Swedish immigrant/small rancher OSKAR HANSON (50s), a gentle man who feels uneasy in this group.

AMOS DRUCKER (40s), a crusty, veteran Army scout of mixed parentage, rides over to Chivington.

> DRUCKER
> Them are peaceable Cheyenne down there, Colonel. No need to attack them.

> CHIVINGTON
> They're hostiles, Mr. Drucker, and I intend to do God's work.

> DRUCKER
> There're women and children down there, Colonel, and they are under the Army's protection.

> CHIVINGTON
> Sir, I am the leader of this expedition. You are an Army scout assigned to me. You will follow my orders.
> (*To Cochran*)
> Mr. Cochran, if this man tries to interfere, shoot him.

COCHRAN
(*Irish accent*)
With pleasure, Colonel.

Cochran, Bedford and Pugh draw their weapons; point them at Drucker.

CHEYENNE CAMP

White Antelope, wearing a headdress, emerges from a teepee, carrying an American flag. He mounts his horse; turns to the anxious Cheyenne, including Running Wolf and Little Butterfly, who surround him.

WHITE ANTELOPE
"They will see their flag and know we wish to live with them in peace."

He rides out toward the ridge.

ATOP THE RIDGE

Chivington, Drucker and others watch White Antelope ride in their direction.

DRUCKER
See, Colonel! That's White Antelope. He's carryin' an American flag.

CHIVINGTON
(*Ignoring him; calls:*)
Prepare to fire!

The cannon crew gets ready to fire its weapon.

DRUCKER
Colonel!

BEDFORD
Colonel told ya to shut up!

Bedford hits Drucker across the back of the head with the butt of his revolver. Drucker falls off his horse, unconscious.

CHIVINGTON
(*Raises arm; to cannon crew*)
Fire!

The cannon FIRES.

CHEYENNE CAMP

The cannon ball explodes several feet away from White Antelope. Furious, the Cheyenne chief tosses the flag onto the ground.

Behind him, Little Butterfly and the other women watch, terrified. Running Wolf and the other men grab their old rifles, bows and other inadequate weapons.

ATOP THE RIDGE

CHIVINGTON
(*Calls out*)
No quarter, gentlemen! Charge!

His saber high, Chivington spurs his horse, leads his men in a charge down the hill toward the Cheyenne camp. The large contingent of men follow, FIRING at will.

Hanson, reluctantly, rides with the troop, but he does not fire his weapon.

Cochran, Bedford and Pugh race their mounts down the hill, firing their weapons, having a good ol' time.

WHITE ANTELOPE

He is struck in the chest by two bullets; falls off of his horse, dead.

THE FLAG

Chivington's troops ride over the American flag, trampling it into the dust.

CHEYENNE CAMP

As the Militia rides into the camp, firing their weapons, screaming women and children run for cover. Cheyenne braves put up a futile attempt to protect their camp, but are cut down by the overwhelming force.

Cheyenne men, women and children are shot down without mercy.

One woman is stripped naked, raped, then stabbed to death.

Militia members set fire to the teepees.

As one Cheyenne brave is held down and castrated, TROOPER JONES (30), brags:

> TROOPER JONES
> It's gonna make a great tobacco pouch.

ATOP THE RIDGE

A dazed Drucker pushes himself up from the ground; watches the massacre, unable to help. Then, he collapses again.

CHEYENNE CAMP

Hanson rides into the camp; reins his horse. He has yet to fire his weapon; is totally shocked by the slaughter going on around him.

RUNNING WOLF

The young, frightened brave, knife in hand, is crouched against the side of a teepee, not quite sure what to do. Then, he spots Hanson, who seems to be in a like quandary, and he makes a decision.

BACK TO SCENE

Running Wolf, knife in hand, runs out from his hiding place; leaps up at Hanson, knocking him off his horse. The two men go sprawling onto the ground, and with the Cheyenne on top, they struggle for the knife. Hanson is definitely losing.

COCHRAN

He rides up; spots Running Wolf on top of Hanson and FIRES his revolver.

BACK TO SCENE

The bullet grazes Running Wolf's forehead, knocking him unconscious.

Cochran rides off to do some more killing.

Hanson gets to his feet; views the carnage about him, then throws up onto the ground.

A RAVINE

A group of Cheyenne women and children huddle in fear in the rock-filled quarry.

Troopers spot them, FIRE their weapons down at them. Bedford and Pugh are among this group.

THE CAMP

Little Butterfly dashes out from inside a teepee, runs toward a wooded area, then turns and sees:

LITTLE BUTTERFLY'S P.O.V.

A Trooper, saber raised, is riding directly at her.

BACK TO SCENE

Little Butterfly is frozen in her tracks.

The Trooper rides by, beheading her with his saber.

BLACKOUT

EXT. FOREST CLEARING DAY.

Hawk and the rest of the hunting party emerge from the wooded area; move across the clearing. Crazy Buffalo is riding point.

Hawk's mind appears to be elsewhere, as Tall Elk rides up next to him.

> TALL ELK
> "Soars Like a Hawk's thoughts are not here. Are they with Little Butterfly?"

> HAWK
> "Her smile is warm like the rising sun."

> TALL ELK
> "She will make you a good wife... even if Crazy Buffalo is her brother."

> HAWK
> "Crazy Buffalo will not be living in our teepee."

CRAZY BUFFALO

He spots something up ahead.

CRAZY BUFFALO'S P.O.V.

In the distance, across the creek, SMOKE is rising from the Cheyenne camp.

BACK TO SCENE

> CRAZY BUFFALO
> (*Calls to Hawk, etal.*)
> "There is trouble!"

Hawk and the others see the smoke.

> HAWK
> (*Blanches*)
> "Little Butterfly..... "

He kicks his horse; races ahead of the others toward the camp. Crazy Buffalo and the others follow quickly behind him.

EXT. CHEYENNE CAMP. DAY.

Hawk rides into the camp; reins his horse and dismounts.

HAWK'S P.O.V.

Total devastation. Dead and dismembered bodies are everywhere. All the teepees have been burned to the ground. There are only a few survivors, and they are not in the best of shape.

BACK TO SCENE

> HAWK
> (*Screams*)
> "Little Butterfly!"

As Crazy Buffalo and the others arrive on the scene, also reacting with shock and anger, Hawk rushes through the camp, searching. He stops when he sees:

HAWK'S P.O.V.

Corpses of the women and children who were shot down in the ravine.

BACK TO SCENE

Moving more slowly, almost in a daze, Hawk walks through the camp, viewing the ruin. He stops when he sees:

HAWK'S P.O.V.

What is apparently the beheaded body of Little Butterfly.

BACK TO SCENE

There are tears behind Hawk's eyes, but they will not come. He drops to his knees; begins to sing the Cheyenne funeral chant.

Crazy Buffalo and the other members of the hunting party, all feeling various degrees of anguish, approach Hawk, but maintain a discreet distance.

EXT. KIRBYTOWN. DAY.

Stuck out in the middle of a plain, this is not really a town, but more of an extended trading post that services the nearby fort, travelers, plus ranches and farms in the area. On a muddy "street," one long frame building with a wooden sidewalk in front of it houses a general store, saloon/cafe and small hotel. A sign along the building top, reads "Kirby's". Several horses are tied to the hitching post in front.

There is also a livery stable and corral with horses in it and a buckboard parked beside it.

ANNA HANSON (22) stands by the corral, feeding one of the horses. She is an attractive blonde Swedish immigrant who hides her beauty by wearing a man's hat and work clothes. Every now and then, she glances anxiously out toward the prairie...looking for something.

LT. HALL (O.S.)

Miss Hanson....

Anna turns to see LT. ADAM HALL (25), a U.S. Army Cavalry officer, on horseback behind her. A West Point graduate with boyish good looks, Hall is friendly; a gentleman.

                    ANNA
          (*Slight Swedish accent; shyly*)
     Lieutenant....

                    LT. HALL
     In town for supplies?

                    ANNA
     No, I stay here 'til my father come back.

                    LT. HALL
                (*Dismounts*)
     Oh? Where did he go?

                    ANNA
          (*Starts back to the main building*)
     He went with the men to find the Indians that stole our
     horses.

Hall walks beside her, leading his mount.

                    LT. HALL
     Chivington? He went with the Militia?

                    ANNA
     Yes, that is where he went.

                    LT. HALL
     Your father's a good man. He doesn't belong with those
     men.

                    ANNA
     We must get back our horses.

As Hall ties his horse to the hitching post, Anna pauses in front of the general store; looks at a cotton dress that adorns a dummy in the window.

> LT. HALL
> (*Watching her*)
> Pretty dress.

Embarrassed at being caught looking, Anna moves away from the window.

> LT. HALL (*cont'd*)
> I bet you'd look right nice in a dress.

Not quite sure how to respond, Anna moves further away from him.

> ANNA
> I have no time for dresses. My father and me have a ranch to work.

> LT. HALL
> Too bad....'Cause there's a dance at the fort Saturday after next... an' I'd be mighty proud to escort you to it, ma'm.

> ANNA
> (*Taken aback*)
> I...I...

O.S. SOUND of rider approaching fast.

Hall and Anna turn to see:

DRUCKER

He gallops into town.

Behind him, out on the prairie, several other riders approach.

BACK TO SCENE

Drucker spots Hall; reins his horse, stopping next to him.

> DRUCKER
>
> Where's the General?

> LT. HALL
>
> He's in the store, buyin' cigars. What's up?

> DRUCKER
>
> Plenty.

He ties up his horse; rushes into the general store.

> LT. HALL
> (*To Anna*)
> Excuse me, ma'm. I'd better see if the General needs me.

Anna nods; looks out toward the prairie at the approaching riders.

> LT. HALL (*cont'd*)
> I'll check back with you about that dance.

> ANNA
>
> I will think on it.

> LT. HALL
>
> Thank you, ma'm.

Hall enters the store.

Anna looks back toward the prairie, and sees:

HANSON

Shaken by his experience, he enters the town with the other riders.

BACK TO SCENE

Anna steps down into the muddy street; rushes over to her father.

> ANNA
>
> Poppa...are you all right?

HANSON
(*Swedish accent*)
Get the wagon. We will go home now.

They head toward the livery stable.

ANNA
Where are our horses?

Hanson does not answer.

EXT. BEHIND KIRBY'S. DAY.

The back porch/steps of the general store. Drucker, Hall and
GENERAL LAWRENCE C. PARKS (55) emerge from the store.
Parks is tall, bearded; a responsible, fair-minded career officer. He
chews on an unlit cigar.

Hall shuts the door behind them for privacy.

PARKS
(*Appalled*)
A hundred fifty dead!?!

DRUCKER
Close to it. Mostly women and children.

PARKS
Damn that Chivington! Those Cheyenne were under
Government protection. Damn him to Hell!

LT. HALL
What're we going to do, sir?

PARKS
Shoot Chivington. That's what I'd like to do. Shoot the
goddamn governor, too. He's the one that put that Bible-
thumpin' son-of-a-bitch in charge of the state militia.

DRUCKER

That "militia," General, is filled with half the thieves and drifters in the territory.

LT. HALL

Should I put the fort on alert?

PARKS

Oh, yeah. And, we'd better telegraph Washington. They're going want to hear about this one.

EXT. THE PRAIRIE. DAY.

Kirbytown in the distance behind them, the Hansons head their buckboard toward their ranch. Hanson, holding the reins, is silent; stares straight ahead.

ANNA

Poppa, what is wrong?

HANSON

Nothing is wrong.

ANNA
(*Beat*)
What happened out there?
HANSON
(*Snaps*)
Nothing happened! I don't want to talk about it.

Anna, bewildered by her father's reaction, remains silent, as they continue on their journey home.

EXT. KIRBYTOWN. DAY.

Parks, Drucker and Hall emerge from the front of the general store; go to their horses.

PARKS

Drucker, you'd better go start warning some of the ranchers to be on their guard.

DRUCKER

I can't warn 'em all, General.

PARKS

The Lieutenant'll dispatch some men to give you a hand.

LT. HALL

Sir, what about Colonel Chivington?

PARKS

He's not Army. I got no authority over him.
(*Beat*)
The bastard figures that, if he makes himself a reputation as a great Indian fighter, it'll get him elected to Congress.... Well, next time, he won't be facing just women and children. He may have started the biggest Indian war this country's ever seen.

EXT. CHEYENNE CAMP. DUSK.

Hawk, Crazy Buffalo and the others in the hunting party are tending to the wounds, giving water and doing whatever they can for the few survivors of the massacre, most of whom are elderly men and women, plus a few young children.

After wrapping an Old Woman in a buffalo robe, a distraught, angry Hawk looks about the camp and sees:

RUNNING WOLF

The young Cheyenne stands off by himself, a troubled expression on his face.

BACK TO SCENE

Sensing Running Wolf's despair, Hawk walks over to him.

HAWK
"Running Wolf showed great courage today."

RUNNING WOLF
"If I had shown great courage, I would be with my ancestors."

HAWK
"If the Wise One Above had wanted Running Wolf to join him in his abode, he would be there."

RUNNING WOLF
"There were so many of them. I tried...."

HAWK
"I have been there myself, little brother. You bear no shame."

Crazy Buffalo, Tall Elk and Yellow Moccasin approach Hawk.

CRAZY BUFFALO
"Does Soars Like a Hawk still wish to be a friend to the white man, or will he be a Cheyenne?"

HAWK
"I am a Cheyenne. A Cheyenne warrior chief...and this murder of our people will not go unpunished."
(*Beat*)
"Ride to the camps of our brother Cheyenne. Tell them to meet us in council...so that we can plan our revenge on the white dogs who did this."

Crazy Buffalo and the others nod approval; go to get their horses.

HAWK (*cont'd*)
(*To Running Wolf*)
"You, little brother, have seen these white men. You will help us find them. That, I think, is why the Wise One Above has spared you."

RUNNING WOLF
"I will find them. And, I will kill them."

SMASH CUT TO:

AN ARROW

It flies through the air toward its target.

TROOPER JONES

He is drinking coffee from a tin cup.

The only illumination is from a CAMPFIRE.

A THUD, as the arrow hits its target.

A look of surprise crosses Jones' face. He opens his mouth and blood spills from it.

He looks down at his midsection to see the point and shaft of the arrow protruding from it.

EXT. CAMPSITE. NIGHT.

Jones and a dozen other Troopers (all in their 20s) who were at Sand Creek have been sitting around a campfire, eating the evening meal.

The other Troopers are momentarily stunned, as Jones' corpse pitches forward onto the ground.

TROOPER
Oh, Jesus Christ!

Cheyenne WAR CRIES from the darkness surrounding them. GUNSHOTS.

Two other Troopers are hit; go down.

The remaining Troopers are disoriented. They grab their weapons; FIRE wildly.

Suddenly, several Cheyenne braves, including Hawk, Crazy Buffalo, Tall Elk, Yellow Moccasin and Running Wolf, burst out of the darkness; attack the Troopers with knives.

Most of the Troopers try to flee.

HAWK

With a vengeance, he buries his knife into the gut of one Trooper, then withdraws the weapon; grabs another Trooper from behind and cuts his throat.

CRAZY BUFFALO

He chases down a fleeing Trooper; tackles him, cuts his throat, then takes his scalp. He stands; gives a Cheyenne cry of victory.

RUNNING WOLF

He leaps at a Trooper who has been able to get onto his horse. The two men go sprawling onto the ground with the Cheyenne winding up on top.

A crazed look in his eyes, Running Wolf plunges his knife into the Trooper's chest, again and again and again...long after the man is dead.

ANOTHER TROOPER

He has been able to get to his horse and is attempting to get away.

HAWK

He spots the man, grabs one of the trooper's rifles, takes aim and FIRES.

ANOTHER TROOPER

The man falls from the horse, dead.

BACK TO SCENE

The battle has ended. Hawk and the other Cheyenne survey the bloody scene. All of the Troopers are dead. No Cheyenne have been hurt.

Hawk sees:

RUNNING WOLF

He is still on top of the Trooper; still plunging his knife into the dead body.

BACK TO SCENE

Hawk walks over to Running Wolf; places his hand on his shoulder.

> HAWK
> "That is enough, little brother."

Running Wolf stops; looks up at Hawk. His expression is a mix of anger, bewilderment, relief and sadness.

> HAWK (*cont'd*)
> "You have shown the courage of a warrior this day."

> RUNNING WOLF
> (*Stands*)
> "I will not be a true warrior until they are all dead."

SMASH CUT TO:

EXT. THE PRAIRIE. DAY.

A Paymaster's wagon, with a guard of perhaps two dozen troopers accompanying it, rolls across the plains.

HAWK

Followed by Crazy Buffalo, Running Wolf and the rest of his guerrilla band, he rides to the top of a hill that overlooks the caravan.

He gestures that they should attack.

BACK TO SCENE

The Cheyenne attack. The Troopers take cover in nearby brush.

The Cheyenne set fire to the brush.

RUNNING WOLF

He FIRES his rifle at the troopers with a mad vengeance.

HAWK

He FIRES his Henry rife at the Troopers.

BACK TO SCENE

As the Cheyenne swarm over them, the Troopers are defeated.

SMASH CUT TO:

EXT. HANSON RANCH. DAY.

Located at the base of a tall cliff.

A small ranch house, a barn, corral, well and privy, surrounded by some trees; stuck out in the middle of nowhere. A few horses are in the corral; some cattle grazing nearby. A vegetable garden and a very small cornfield is near the house.

About a hundred yards from the ranch yard is a shallow gully.

Anna, still dressed in male clothing, and Hanson are doing some repair work on the corral. With Hanson's mind back at Sand Creek and just going through the motions, Anna is definitely "in charge" of this project. He holds the board, while she hammers in the nails.

ANNA
(*Checking her pockets*)
We need more nails.

HANSON
(*Beat*)
I get them.

ANNA
Hold the board, Poppa. I get them.

She goes into the barn.

ATOP THE CLIFF

Hawk, Running Wolf, Crazy Buffalo and the rest of the Cheyenne band ride to the edge of the cliff; look down at the Hanson Ranch.

CHEYENNE P.O.V.

Hanson is alone; holding the board. He is not recognizable from this distance.

ATOP THE CLIFF

CRAZY BUFFALO
"We should attack from two sides. I will take...."

HAWK
(*Interrupts*)
"Wait!"
(*To Running Wolf*)
"Do you know him?"

RUNNING WOLF
(*Shrugs*)
"He is too far."

CRAZY BUFFALO
"What difference? He is a white man!"

                    HAWK
          (*Ponders a moment, then he nods
            agreement to Crazy Buffalo:*)
      "Take Tall Elk...two others...ride down to the other side
      of...."

He stops when he sees:

HAWK'S P.O.V.

Anna emerges from the barn, walks to the corral.

RANCH YARD

As Anna nears the corral, she takes off her hat, exposing her long
blonde hair. She wipes her forehead with the back of her hand.

ATOP THE CLIFF

                    HAWK
      "That is a woman."

                CRAZY BUFFALO
      "A white woman."

                    HAWK
      "We do not make war on women."

                CRAZY BUFFALO
      "At Sand Creek, the whites made war on our women...and
      children."

                    HAWK
      "We are not the whites."

RANCH YARD

Hanson glances up and sees:

HANSON'S P.O.V.

The Cheyenne atop the cliff.

BACK TO SCENE

> HANSON
> (*Blanches*)
> Oh, Mother of God!

Anna turns and also sees the Cheyenne.

> ANNA
> (*In charge*)
> Poppa...where is the rifle?

> HANSON
> In the house.

Anna moves toward the house. Hanson does not move; just stares up at the cliff.

> ANNA
> Poppa! Come!

Hanson starts after her. Anna continues toward the house, then stops when she sees:

ANNA'S P.O.V.

The Cheyenne are leaving. Only Hawk does not move.

BACK TO SCENE

> ANNA
> They are leaving, Poppa.

HAWK

As the other Cheyenne depart, he continues to watch Anna. There is something familiar about her; something that evokes a memory.

ANNA

She continues to watch the lone Cheyenne atop the cliff. Despite the distance between them, they are "making contact".

ANNA'S P.O.V.

Hawk finally turns his horse; disappears from sight.

RANCH YARD

The Hansons continue to watch the cliff.

> HANSON
> Why they go? They have been killing whites all over the territory.

> ANNA
> I don't know.

DISSOLVE TO:

EXT. ARMY CAMP. DAY.

Establishing shot. An encampment of tents for a well equipped U.S. Army regiment. They are preparing to go out to fight the Cheyenne.

INT. GENERAL PARK'S TENT. DAY.

Coat unbuttoned, Parks sits behind his desk, reviewing some documents; smoking a cigar.

Lieutenant Hall enters.

> LT. HALL
> We've found him, General.

> PARKS
> Drucker? Where?

LT. HALL
He was in Kirby's saloon.

PARKS
(*Ponders a moment*)
Well, bring 'im in.

LT. HALL
(*Calls*)
Sergeant!

SGT. BATES (35), burly, a career soldier, enters holding onto Drucker's arm. The scout is somewhat disheveled; has had enough drinks to loosen his tongue.

The Sergeant seats Drucker in a chair in front of the General's desk; takes a position by the tent entrance. Hall stands at Parks' side.

PARKS
Mr. Drucker....Where've you been these past months?

DRUCKER
Thought I'd see me the Pacific Ocean.

PARKS
(*Studies him; puffs cigar*)
And what did you think of it?

DRUCKER
Big.

PARKS
That it is....I got a job for you.

DRUCKER
I don't work for the Army no more.

PARKS
Kirby's rotgut is not going to make Sand Creek go away.

DRUCKER
I don't work for the Army no more.

PARKS
Sometimes I wish I didn't work for it either...but I got a job to do and, like it or not, you're going to help me do it.

DRUCKER
Why me?

PARKS
Because your father was a German trader and your mother was the daughter of a Sioux chief.

DRUCKER
I'm not the only half-breed in the territory.

PARKS
No...but I hear you've had dealings with a Cheyenne warrior chief named Soars Like a Hawk.

DRUCKER
I know Hawk. What about him?

PARKS
While you've been out admiring the Pacific Ocean, this Hawk and his band of Cheyenne have been raiding ranches, killing dozens of whites....

DRUCKER
Militia?

PARKS
Mostly.

DRUCKER
Good for them.

PARKS

We've even posted a reward for him, but....

DRUCKER

That ain't gonna do you no good.

PARKS

I know, but it has to stop. That's why I need you.

DRUCKER

You expect me to talk him into surrendering?
(*Laughs*)
And why would he do that?

PARKS

Because you'll convince him that there's no viable
alternative.

Drucker has no immediate response. He ponders the General's
words.

EXT. KIRBYTOWN. DAY.

A handbill, offering $1000.00 reward for Soars Like a Hawk, has
been posted on a bulletin board outside the saloon.

Cochran, Bedford and Pugh emerge from the saloon.

COCHRAN

(*Angry; calls back into saloon*)
You're a son-of-a-bitch, Kirby... not extendin' credit to three
honest members of the Colorado Militia.

PUGH

(*Parrots him; shouts*)
Son-of-a-bitch!

DRUCKER

He emerges from the general store with his saddlebags, which he puts over his horse. He pays no attention to Cochran and his group.

BACK TO SCENE

                    COCHRAN
                  (*Sees handbill*)
        Would you look at this. They're offerin' a thousand dollar
        reward fer that murderin' redskin.

                    BEDFORD
        Could use that thousand dollars.

                    COCHRAN
        Back in County Cork, they were only offerin' twenty quid
        fer me....What kind of world is it that values a bloody Injun
        over a fine strappin' Irishman?

Cochran glances toward the street, and sees:

COCHRAN'S P.O.V.

Drucker is riding out of town toward the prairie.

BACK TO SCENE

                    COCHRAN
        Billy, me lad, go back into Kirby's and get a couple of the
        boys.

                    BEDFORD
        What's up?

                    COCHRAN
        I think I got us way to collect that thousand dollars.

As Bedford re-enters the saloon, Cochran continues to watch Drucker depart.

EXT. THE PRAIRIE. DAY.

In a SERIES OF SHOTS, Drucker rides along the desolate plain. He carries a pole with a feather arrangement atop it.

EXT. THE PRAIRIE. NIGHT.

Drucker sits alone at a campfire, drinking coffee; eating from a can of beans.

EXT. CANYON. DAY.

Drucker rides through the canyon, still carrying the pole. He reins his horse; takes a drink from his canteen.

> HAWK (*O.S.*)
> Drucker!

Drucker does not turn around.

> DRUCKER
> Hello, Hawk.

He takes another drink from his canteen.

Hawk sits on his horse, several yards behind the scout. The Henry is cradled across his lap.

> HAWK
> You are either very foolish or very brave.

> DRUCKER
> (*Still does not look at him*)
> Hell, I knew you were watching me since yesterday.

He turns his horse to face Hawk.

> HAWK
> Did you also know that my brothers wanted to kill you?

Drucker looks about and sees:

DRUCKER'S P.O.V.

Crazy Buffalo, Running Wolf and other Cheyenne are atop the cliff, their weapons pointed at him.

BACK TO SCENE

> DRUCKER
> Figured that. I also figured that you'd want to hear what I had to say.

Hawk kicks his horse; moves closer to Drucker.

> HAWK
> You ride with the whites.

> DRUCKER
> Yeah, I do. But, I also ride with the Cheyenne...the Sioux...the Arapaho....You are all my brothers.

> HAWK
> (*Beat*)
> Come. We will talk.

Hawk kicks his horse; moves past Drucker, who follows.

EXT. HAWK'S CAMP. DAY.

Located in a hidden part of the canyon, with high boulders surrounding it and limited access, the camp is a natural fortress.

Hawk, Crazy Buffalo, Tall Elk and Drucker stand/pace in a heated powwow at one end of the camp, while behind them Running Wolf, Yellow Moccasin and the other Cheyenne watch and stand guard.

> HAWK
> When the last white who was at Sand Creek is dead, then we will talk of peace.

DRUCKER
I was at Sand Creek. Are you going to kill me, too?

Crazy Buffalo cocks his rifle; points it at Drucker.

HAWK
You were at Sand Creek?

DRUCKER
I tried to stop it. Got hit on the head. When I came to, it was over.

CRAZY BUFFALO
He lies! Kill him!

He gets ready to shoot Drucker. Tall Elk draws his knife.

HAWK
If he lied, he would not be here.

TALL ELK
(*To Drucker*)
You are part Indian. Why do you ride with the whites who did this?

DRUCKER
The whites I ride with were not at Sand Creek.
(*To Hawk*)
The leaders in Washington say that Sand Creek was a national tragedy... a disgrace. They want to make amends to the Cheyenne.

HAWK
(*Sarcastic*)
How would they do that? Will they bring back Crazy Buffalo's sister... my bride-to-be?

DRUCKER

I....

HAWK

Will they punish the men responsible?

DRUCKER

The territorial governor...the man who appointed
Chivington...has been forced to resign, and Colonel
Chivington ....He's run off to California someplace.
Legally, they can't touch him.

HAWK

They are alive, and the women and children of Sand Creek
are dead.

DRUCKER

They are alive.

HAWK

Then, how will the leaders in Washington make "amends"?

DRUCKER

Chief Black Kettle has accepted the Government's offer to
move the Cheyenne to a reservation in the Oklahoma
Territory. They'll be given cattle, taught how to grow their
own food....

HAWK

They will be fed like dogs.

CRAZY BUFFALO

The Cheyenne eat their dogs.

DRUCKER

The white man's war in the East will be ending soon. Many
blue coats... with greater weapons... will be coming West.
If Soars Like a Hawk and his brothers fight them, they will
be destroyed.

                    HAWK
Many blue coats will also die.

                   DRUCKER
General Parks will grant you and your brothers amnesty...if
you will lay down your weapons and join Black Kettle on
the reservation.

                    HAWK
                   (*Beat*)
Generals lie.

                   DRUCKER
I believe this one speaks the truth.
                   (*Beat*)
Hawk, what was that story you told me once about the
mountain lion and the grizzly bear?

                    HAWK
                   (*Beat*)
The mountain lion is wise. He does not attack a stronger
foe like the grizzly bear. He avoids him.

                   DRUCKER
Well, this grizzly bear in the blue coat ain't gonna be
avoided....You can fight 'im, but, in the end, he's going to
win....Or, you can help your people. Black Kettle's getting
old.   The Cheyenne are going to need a strong leader like
you if they're going to survive.

Hawk ponders Drucker's words.

EXT. THE PRAIRIE. DAY.

Drucker and Hawk, followed by Crazy Buffalo, Tall Elk, Running
Wolf and the rest of the Cheyenne head back across the plain toward
Kirbytown. As they approach a rock and tree covered hill, Crazy
Buffalo rides up next to Hawk.

CRAZY BUFFALO
(*Indicating Drucker*)
This man is not to be trusted. He is leading us into a trap.

DRUCKER
It's no trap.

HAWK
I will hear the white general's words...look into his eyes...then I will decide.

CRAZY BUFFALO
Soars Like a Hawk has still not decided if his heart is with the whites or the Cheyenne.

As the group starts up the hill, an angry Crazy Buffalo turns his horse; re-joins the rest of the Cheyenne behind Hawk and Drucker.

DRUCKER
Angry fella, ain't he?

HAWK
If Crazy Buffalo misses a buffalo with his arrow, he gets angry at the buffalo. That's why he is called Crazy Buffalo.

DRUCKER
I'm going to leave you here at the top of the rise...go an' bring back the General. You'll be able to see four...five miles. Make sure we're not bein' followed.

HAWK
Good.

DRUCKER
I think you'll like the General. He's a square shooter....

An O.S. GUNSHOT.

Drucker is hit in the chest; falls off his horse, dead.

40

More O.S. GUNSHOTS.

Yellow Moccasin is hit, killed.

Two other Cheyenne braves are also killed. One of them falls from his horse, tumbles down the embankment.

COCHRAN & COMPANY

He, Bedford, Pugh and two other reprobates, who we will call FRANK and BART (both in their 20s), are positioned at various spots atop the hill, FIRING their rifles down at the Cheyenne.

HAWK

His horse is hit by a bullet. It rears up, then stumbles. Hawk is thrown off; tumbles down the embankment. At the bottom, his head hits a rock and he's knocked unconscious.

RUNNING WOLF

He sees what has happened to Hawk. Jumps off his horse; slides down the embankment after him.

BACK TO SCENE

More O.S. GUNSHOTS. Tall Elk is killed.

COCHRAN AND BEDFORD

They continue to shoot at the Cheyenne.

                    BEDFORD
          Which one is Soars Like a Hawk?

                    COCHRAN
          Damned if I know.

BACK TO SCENE

Crazy Buffalo takes cover behind a rock. BULLETS RICOCHET off the rock, as he takes aim with his rifle; FIRES.

FRANK

He's hit; comes tumbling down the hill, dead.

COCHRAN AND BEDFORD

> BEDFORD
> That son-of-a-bitch!

As Cochran draws a bead on Crazy Buffalo:

> COCHRAN
> Don't be frettin' about ol' Frank there.

He FIRES his rifle.

CRAZY BUFFALO

He's hit in the forehead; falls dead.

COCHRAN AND BEDFORD

> COCHRAN
> (*Lowering his rifle*)
> That's one less split of the reward money.

BACK TO SCENE

All of the Cheyenne are dead. Anxious and/or dead horses are next to their fallen riders.

BOTTOM OF THE HILL

Hawk, still unconscious, lies behind a boulder, hidden from sight. Running Wolf kneels over him, trying to shake him awake. The young Cheyenne looks up the hill, and sees:

RUNNING WOLF'S P.O.V.

Cochran and his men have emerged from their hiding places; are checking the bodies of their victims.

RUNNING WOLF

Realizing that he can do nothing for Hawk now, the young brave, knife in hand, creeps up the embankment toward the whites.

BACK TO SCENE

Bedford turns over the body of a dead Cheyenne. Running Wolf creeps up behind him, ready to attack with his knife.

As Running Wolf gets ready to stab the unaware bounty hunter:

Cochran steps up behind Running Wolf; hits him on the back of the head with his rifle butt. The young Cheyenne drops, unconscious.

> BEDFORD
> (*Startled*)

Jesus Christ!

> COCHRAN

You need eyes in the back of your head with these redskins, Billy, me boy.

Bedford takes out his revolver; gets ready to shoot Running Wolf.

> COCHRAN (*cont'd*)

No, don't kill 'em.
> (*Calls to Pugh*)

Brian, get me some rope.

PUGH

As he goes for the rope, he spots Hawk's Henry rifle, lying on the ground by the dead horse.

BACK TO SCENE

Cochran kicks Running Wolf, who is starting to come around.

> COCHRAN
> (*To Running Wolf*)
> Wake up, ya little bastard. Which one of these dead bucks is your.... What do ya call 'im?...Soarin' Hawk?

> RUNNING WOLF
> (*Dazed; in Cheyenne*)
> "Fuck you."

> COCHRAN
> (*Kicks him again; in Cheyenne*)
> "Same to you."
> (*In English*)
> Now, which one is he?

> RUNNING WOLF
> (*Beat; In English*)
> He is not here.

> COCHRAN
> Then, bucko, unless you want me to cut off yer balls for a new tobacco pouch, you're gonna take us to him.

The threat definitely frightens the young Cheyenne.

DISSOLVE TO:

EXT. BOTTOM OF HILL. DUSK.

Hawk, still lying behind the boulder, awakens; looks about.

HAWK'S P.O.V.

He is intermittently seeing double.

BACK TO SCENE

Hawk shakes his head. He notes that his only weapon is his knife.
With some difficulty, he starts climbing back up the embankment.

He reaches the top of the incline and sees:

HAWK'S P.O.V.

The dead bodies of Drucker and the Cheyenne lie about. Running
Wolf is not among them. Horses, weapons and anything else of
value are gone.

BACK TO SCENE

Hawk raises his arms; screams in anger/anguish to the Wise One
Above.

DISSOLVE TO:

EXT. THE PRAIRIE. NIGHT.

Hawk stumbles along in the darkness, heading back in the direction
of his canyon camp. He looks up at the stars above; chooses a
direction, then proceeds.

EXT. COCHRAN'S CAMPSITE. NIGHT.

Cochran, Bedford, Pugh and Bart sit around the campfire, eating.
Running Wolf is tied to a nearby tree.

Cochran notices the Henry rifle next to Pugh.

COCHRAN
Brian, me lad, where did you get that lovely Henry?

PUGH
Belonged to one of them Injuns.

COCHRAN

Toss it here.

PUGH

It's mine.

COCHRAN

I just want to take a look at it.

Pugh, reluctantly, tosses Cochran the rifle, who examines it.

COCHRAN (*cont'd*)

I hear tell that that Soarin' Hawk Injun had him a Henry.

He looks over at Running Wolf.

EXT. WOODED AREA. DAY.

Hawk, still groggy from his injury, as well as a lack of food and sleep, comes across a stream. He falls to his knees; drinks. Suddenly, he stops drinking and listens.

O.S. SOUND of approaching horses.

Hawk scrambles away from the stream; conceals himself behind a thick stand of trees. He listens and watches.

HAWK'S P.O.V.

A six-man Pawnee Hunting Party approaches the stream from the opposite direction. They drink; allow their horses to drink. Onlytwo of the Pawnee, including RED BEAR (30), their leader, have rifles. The others are armed with bow-and arrow.

HAWK

Staying low, grips his knife.

HAWK'S P.O.V.

Red Bear finishes drinking from the stream and is about to remount his horse when, suddenly he gazes into the trees in Hawk's direction. Has he spotted him?

HAWK

He doesn't move; grips his knife harder.

HAWK'S P.O.V.

Red Bear continues to stare.

HAWK

Hawk continues to stay low.

> WHITE BULL (*O.S.*)
> He will not see you.

Knife ready, Hawk spins around and sees:

HAWK'S P.O.V.

WHITE BULL, a very old Cheyenne Medicine Man sits in the shadows behind Hawk, leaning against a tree. [NOTE: During this scene, White Bull is only seen from Hawk's slightly blurred P.O.W.]

BACK TO SCENE

> HAWK
> You're White Bull, the medicine man.

> WHITE BULL
> I am White Bull.

> HAWK
> I remember you when I was a young brave.

He glances back at Red Bear.

WHITE BULL
He will not see you.

Though he has great respect for holy men like White Bull, Hawk is somewhat dubious.

HAWK
Have you cast a spell to make us invisible?

WHITE BULL
(*Shakes head; indicates Red Bear*)
Eyes bad. Need pieces of glass some white men wear.

RED BEAR

He continues to stare in Hawk's direction for a few more tense moments, then remounts his horse. He and the other five Pawnee head off away from Hawk.

BACK TO SCENE

Hawk waits until the Pawnee are out of sight; turns back to White Bull.

WHITE BULL
I have been waiting for you, Soars Like a Hawk.

HAWK
You remember me?

WHITE BULL
I have not forgotten you.

HAWK
White Bull went on a vision quest. He did not return.

WHITE BULL
My heart was old.

Hawk is not sure if he is hallucinating.

WHITE BULL (*cont'd*)
The spirits have shown me that Soars Like a Hawk will be a savior of the Cheyenne.

HAWK
(*Doesn't believe him*)
A savior?

WHITE BULL
Your journey will be long. You will lead our people in battle against the Pawnee...whites...other enemies, but you will also help to forge a bridge of peace.

HAWK
How can this be? My brothers are dead.

WHITE BULL
(*Ignoring question*)
Before this can happen, you must first forge a bridge of peace within yourself.

These final words hit home with Hawk. He ponders them for several moments, then turns back to White Bull.

The old medicine man has disappeared.

Hawk scrambles to his feet; looks about, but White Bull is gone. Suddenly, Hawk's weakened condition gets the best of him. He passes out onto the ground.

EXT. AMBUSH SITE. DAY.

Cochran, Bedford and Pugh are looking over the bodies of the dead Cheyenne. Running Wolf, hands tied behind his back, has a short rope around his neck, the other end being held, like a leash, by Cochran.

COCHRAN
(*To Running Wolf*)
Which one is he?

RUNNING WOLF
(*Points to Crazy Buffalo's body*)

Him.

COCHRAN
(*Slugs him*)

Don't be lyin' to me, you little bastard.
(*Points to the dead horse*)
Brian found the Henry over there.

BART (*O.S.*)
(*Calls*)

Jimmy!

Cochran pulls Running Wolf over to the edge of the embankment.
Bedford joins him.

Bart is at the bottom of the embankment, standing by the bolder that
hid Hawk.

BART (*cont'd*)
(*Calls*)

There's blood on the rock here.

COCHRAN
(*Thinking out loud; to Bedford*)

So, his horse got shot....He fell down the bank....Maybe got
knocked out...and crawled away....Now, which way would
he go?

EXT. WOODED AREA. DAY.

Hawk awakens, feeling greatly refreshed. He recalls his encounter
with White Bull; looks about, not quite sure if the medicine man was
real or a dream. Looking upward, he sees:

HAWK'S P.O.V.

The medicine man's long dead remains lie in a tree above him, but
his clothing make him instantly recognizable.

BACK TO SCENE

Hawk is taken aback by his discovery. He ponders his experience for a long moment, then slowly moves on.

DISSOLVE TO:

EXT. ABOVE THE HANSON RANCH. DUSK.

Hawk arrives at the cliff that overlooks the ranch; crouches down.

HAWK'S P.O.V.

The ranch yard is empty, except for the horses in the corral. A lamplight is on in the house; smoke is coming from the chimney.

BACK TO SCENE

Hawk starts to make his way down the cliff.

EXT. HANSON RANCH. DUSK.

Hawk reaches the bottom of the cliff; stealthily makes his way to the barn; goes inside.

INT. BARN. DUSK.

Hawk leaves the door slightly ajar to let in the light. He looks about; spots the corn crib. He goes to it, takes a piece or corn; eats hungrily.

EXT. HANSON RANCH. DUSK.

Anna comes out of the ranch house, carrying a water bucket. She goes to the well. As she fills the bucket, she glances up and sees:

ANNA'S P.O.V.

The barn door is partly open.

BACK TO SCENE

Anna leaves the bucket at the well; goes to the barn to close the door.

INT. BARN. DUSK.

Anna takes a step inside to make sure everything is okay, sees:

ANNA'S P.O.V.

Hawk, at the corn crib, is eating a second piece of corn. He sees her.

BACK TO SCENE

Startled, Anna emits a involuntary scream.

INT. RANCH HOUSE. DUSK.

Hanson, who has been reading his Bible, hears the scream.

INT. BARN. DUSK.

Anna is frozen to her spot. Hawk stares at her for a moment, perhaps remembering something, then:

>HAWK
>I will not hurt you.

Anna doesn't move. He takes a step toward her.

>HAWK (*cont'd*)
>I take food. Horse. Go.

He raises his hands slightly to show he means her no harm, as he moves past her.

Their eyes meet. Though she is frightened, there is a definite "connection" between them.

EXT. RANCH YARD. DUSK.

Hawk emerges from the barn, watching Anna, who is still just inside the door.

O.S. SOUND of a rifle being cocked.

Hawk turns and sees:

HAWK'S P.O.V.

Hanson stands a few feet away, shakily pointing his rifle at him.

> HANSON
>
> Where is my Anna?

BACK TO SCENE

Hawk keeps his hands half raised, as Anna steps out of the barn.

> HANSON
> (*Lowers rifle*)
> Anna, are you all right?

Anna nods.

Hawk seizes the moment; leaps forward to snatch the rifle from Hanson. For a brief instant, he considers shooting Hanson, but then, aware of Anna's presence:

> HAWK
>
> I take rifle, too.

Anna, suddenly, forgets her fear; get angry.

> ANNA
>
> No!

She steps forward; slaps Hawk hard across the face. He is totally taken aback by her action.

ANNA (*cont'd*)
That's our rifle. Our horse.

HANSON
Anna, no...!

He steps forward grabs his daughter.

HANSON (*cont'd*)
(*To Hawk*)
Take the rifle. Take the horse. I give them to you. Just go.

Hawk, somewhat bewildered and intrigued by Anna's action, starts toward the corral, then stops; turns back toward them.

HAWK
(*Angry*)
No! I no take gifts from white man.

Suddenly, he sees something; raises the rifle; points it in their direction and FIRES.

The bullet whizzes past the Hansons. Startled, they turn and see.

PAWNEE BRAVE

From Red Bear's hunting party. He had been standing a few feet behind Hanson, ready to fire his rifle. Hit in the chest by Hawk's shot, he falls dead.

BACK TO SCENE

The Hansons are bewildered at what just happened.

HAWK
He Pawnee.

Suddenly, another Pawnee, knife in hand, leaps out from the darkness over the top of the corral onto Hawk's back. Hawk drops the rifle and the two men go sprawling.

They roll around on the ground together, with the Pawnee, due to Hawk's weakened condition, getting the best of it. The Pawnee gets on top; Hawk holding back the knife from plunging into his chest.

Hanson snatches up the rifle; not quite sure what to do with it. Anna notes her father's indecision; grabs the rifle from him. She steps forward and smashes the Pawnee across the back of the head with the rifle butt.

The Pawnee falls back, dazed. Hawk grabs the opportunity to snatch up the knife; plunge it into his adversary's chest.

He looks at Anna, somewhat surprised at what she has done.

She appears somewhat surprised at what she has done, also.

An arrow suddenly shoots out from the darkness, hitting Hanson in the shoulder. He screams in pain; falls to the ground.

> ANNA
> (*Screams*)
> Poppa!

As she runs to help her father, Hawk snatches the rifle from her. He spins around, spots the third Pawnee getting ready to shoot another arrow, and FIRES.

The Pawnee is hit; falls dead.

Hawk looks about for other Pawnee.

Anna tries to get her father up, but he's too heavy.

> ANNA (*cont'd*)
> (*To Hawk*)
> Please help me.

Keeping his eye out for other Pawnee, Hawk goes to Hanson. He hands Anna the rifle.

HAWK
(*Indicating darkness*)
You watch.

Anna keeps one eye out for other Pawnee, while she watches Hawk break the arrow that is stuck in her father's shoulder. Hanson screams in pain.

Hawk picks up Hanson; carries him toward the ranch house. Anna follows, covering their retreat with the rifle.

INT. RANCH HOUSE. DUSK.

It's a one-room structure; a fireplace, two beds; simple handmade furniture with a few small items that betray the fact that the occupants are originally from Sweden.

Hawk enters, carrying Hanson, followed by Anna who shuts/bolts the door behind them.

ANNA
Put him on the bed.

Hawk carries Hanson to the bed; puts him down. Hanson screams in pain.

HAWK
White man scream like a woman.

ANNA
(*Snaps, as she goes to her father*)
Have you ever been shot with an arrow?
HAWK
Two times.

Anna looks at Hanson's wound; doesn't really know what to do. She looks at Hawk, hoping that he will help.

HAWK (*cont'd*)
"Fights Like a Man Woman" need help again?

Anna nods.

> HAWK (*cont'd*)
> (*Indicates window*)
> You watch for Pawnee.

Anna takes the rifle; goes to the window to watch.

Hawk moves over to Hanson, examines his wound, then, with care, pulls the arrow out of his shoulder. Instead of screaming this time, Hanson slips into unconsciousness.

From her post at the window, Anna watches him.

Using his knife, Hawk cuts a piece of cloth from Hanson's shirt; uses it to bandage the wound.

> HAWK (*cont'd*)
> (*Goes to Anna*)
> He sleep. Get better.

He takes the rifle from her.

> HAWK (*cont'd*)
> Sit with him.

> ANNA
> Thank you.

> HAWK
> (*Grunts*)
> Me hate Pawnee more than white man.

She goes to her father; sits on the edge of the bed.

> ANNA
> Do you think they're gone?

> HAWK
> Maybe. Three more somewhere.

> ANNA

They want our horses?

Hawk nods; grunts.

> ANNA (*cont'd*)

You were going to steal a horse, too.

> HAWK

White man take Cheyenne land. Kill Cheyenne buffalo.
Maybe Cheyenne sometimes take white man's horses.
> (*Beat*)

You talk funny for white woman.

> ANNA

We're from Sweden.

> HAWK

Sweden?

> ANNA

It's....It's across the big ocean.

> HAWK

"Fights Like a Man Woman" should take father and go
back across big ocean.

> ANNA

We are staying right here on our ranch....And, my name is
Anna.

> HAWK

Anna.

> ANNA

Your name?

> HAWK

I am Soars Like a Hawk.

> ANNA

Soars...?

> HAWK

Hawk.

> *(Beat)*

All women in Sweden dress like men?

> ANNA

I dress like this because I do work with my father on the ranch. Hard work.

> HAWK

Cheyenne women do hard work. They dress like women. Better you dress like woman, too.

He turns away from her; looks out the window.

Pondering his words, Anna turns back to her father.

EXT. HANSON RANCH. DAWN.

Except for the three dead Pawnee that are still in the ranch yard, everything appears normal. A Pawnee horse is behind the barn.

INT. RANCH HOUSE. DAWN.

Hanson is asleep on the bed. Anna is asleep in a rocking chair next to him. As the MORNING SUN hits her face and hair, she opens her eyes, and sees:

HAWK

He sits on the floor beneath the window, staring at her.

BACK TO SCENE

> ANNA
> *(Startled)*

What?

HAWK

You handsome woman.

ANNA
(*Embarrassed*)

Well...I....

HAWK

I know white woman with yellow hair once.

ANNA

Many white women have...yellow hair.

HAWK

This woman my friend.

ANNA

What happened to her?

HAWK

She go to Oregon with other whites. That is where she belong.
(*Beat*)
If Anna and her father smart, they will leave Cheyenne land. Go to Oregon, too.

ANNA

We're not going back to Sweden and we're not going to Oregon. This is our home. We're staying here.

HANSON

He opens his eyes; listens to the conversation.

BACK TO SCENE

HAWK

I think Anna need husband. Maybe if she go to Oregon and dress like woman, she find one.

                    ANNA
I don't need a husband.

                    HAWK
Father not strong. What you do when he not here?

                    ANNA
My father will be here!

Hawk does not respond; turns from her and looks out the window.

                    ANNA (*cont'd*)
                    (*Beat*)
You're the one the soldiers are looking for.

                    HAWK
I am the one.

                    ANNA
If this white woman was your friend, how can you hate
white people so much?

                    HAWK
You know about Sand Creek?

HANSON

The mention of Sand Creek frightens him.

BACK TO SCENE

                    ANNA
Yah....

                    HAWK
What you know?

ANNA

The men...the militia...went out to stop some bad Indians
from raiding our ranches. Those Indians stole some of our
horses.

HAWK

Militia attacked peaceful Cheyenne village. Killed
women... children....My bride-to-be.

ANNA
(*Incredulous*)

No...!

HAWK

When all militia is dead, then maybe I stop hating whites.

ANNA
(*Still unbelieving, she starts to*
point to Hanson)

No, my....

HANSON
(*Interrupts her; frightened*)

Anna...!

ANNA

Poppa, what is it?

HANSON

Water.

ANNA

I get it for you.

She looks about for the water bucket, then remembers.

ANNA (*cont'd*)
(*To Hawk*)
The bucket is by the well.

Hawk looks out the window.

HAWK'S P.O.V.

The ranch yard is quiet.

BACK TO SCENE

Hawk unbolts the door; opens it. Rifle ready, he looks outside, then:

> HAWK
>
> You get water. I watch.

Anna moves to the door.

EXT. HANSON RANCH. DAY.

Hawk moves cautiously out of the house; looks for any Pawnee that might be lurking about. Seeing none, he motions to Anna, who comes out of the house; heads for the well.

THE GULLY

Hiding in the gully outside of the ranch yard are Red Bear and the other two Pawnee. They watch Anna fill the water bucket, then with Hawk covering her, return to the house. Hawk remains outside.

INT. RANCH HOUSE. DAY.

With Hawk keeping watch outside, Anna shuts the door; goes to her father. As she prepares a ladle of water for him:

> HANSON
>
> Anna....

> ANNA
> (*Goes to him*)
>
> Yes, Poppa?

> HANSON
>
> Do not tell him about Sand Creek.

                    ANNA
Poppa, what happened there? You didn't...?

                  HANSON
No. I swear on your Mama's grave. I didn't....I couldn't....

He starts to weep.

                    ANNA
    Poppa....?

                  HANSON
They were killing babies, Anna. Little babies.
                   (*Beat*)
If he knows I was there, he'll kill me.

                    ANNA
                   (*Beat*)
He won't know, Poppa.

EXT. AMBUSH SITE. DAY.

Lt. Hall, Sgt. Bates and eight other Union Soldiers are inspecting the
bodies of Drucker and the Cheyenne.

                  LT. HALL
What do you think happened here, Sergeant?

                 SGT. BATES
Looks to me like Drucker was maybe leadin' these
Cheyenne in, and they got themselves ambushed.

                  LT. HALL
    But, by who?

Bates, baffled, simply shakes his head.

> LT. HALL (*cont'd*)
Pick four men to bring these bodies in. The rest of us....I
want to check out some of the nearby ranches. See if
anybody knows something.

> SGT. BATES
Yes, sir.

EXT. HANSON RANCH. DAY.

Hawk is tying up the Pawnee horse at the corral. He now has both
the Hansons' and the dead Pawnee's rifle.

Anna, trying to hide her anxiety, comes out of the house. They walk
toward each other, meeting at the well.

> HAWK
> (*Indicates horse*)
Pawnee horse.
> (*Hands her her rifle;
> shows her the other one*)
Pawnee rifle.

> ANNA
Good.

> HAWK
Father better?

> ANNA
I think so.

> HAWK
Good....Better I go now.

> ANNA
> (*Beat*)
Can I give you some food?

> HAWK
> I take corn already from barn.

They look at each other for a long moment. He doesn't really want to leave and, in a way, she doesn't want him to go either, but both know that is not possible.

> ANNA
> My father....He is a good man. A gentle man....

> HAWK
> (*Noncommittal*)
> Humph.

> ANNA
> He was different when my Mama was alive....Very strong...very determined....She died from fever on the boat coming to America. I was twelve-years-old....I was afraid he was going to throw himself overboard.
> (*Beat*)
> He needs me to look after him.

Hawk looks at her, not sure why she has told him all this, then:

> HAWK
> You good daughter...but still need husband.

> ANNA
> My father...my Poppa comes first.

Suddenly, an arrow WHISTLES through the air; hits the well, just missing Hawk.

Hawk grabs Anna; pushes her to the ground.

A RIFLE SHOT also hits the well, just above their heads.

INT. RANCH HOUSE. DAY.

Hanson, who had been dozing, opens his eyes.

EXT. RANCH YARD. DAY.

Anna and Hawk are as we last saw them.

> ANNA
>
> Pawnee?

> HAWK
>
> Three.

A Pawnee Brave, carrying bow-and-arrow, emerges from the side of the corral; moves across the ranch yard to get a better shot at Hawk and Anna.

Hawk spots the Pawnee; rolls over onto his back and in a half-sitting position, FIRES his rifle.

The Pawnee is hit; falls dead.

> HAWK (*cont'd*)
>
> Now, two.

Another RIFLE SHOT hits the ground about a foot from Hawk, who rolls back behind the cover of the well.

> HAWK (*cont'd*)
>
> One rifle...in gully.

INT. RANCH HOUSE. DAY.

Frightened by the further gunfire, Hanson pushes himself up from the bed, but he is weak, in pain.

EXT. RANCH YARD. DAY.

Hawk and Anna are as we last saw them.

> HAWK
> (*To Anna*)
>
> You good with rifle?

                    ANNA
I've only shot rabbits.

                    HAWK
Now, maybe you shoot Pawnee.
          (*He gets ready to bolt*)
You watch.

Hawk suddenly bolts from behind the well; races toward the corral.

Another RIFLE SHOT just misses him, as he runs; dives behind the corral.

THE GULLY

Red Bear, alone in the gully, swears in Pawnee; reloads his rifle.

BACK TO SCENE

Crawling on his belly, Hawk works his way around to the far side of the corral.

ANNA

Rifle ready, she watches Hawk's progress.

RANCH HOUSE ROOF

A Pawnee Brave, armed with bow-and-arrow, climbs up onto the roof from the opposite side of the house.

BACK TO SCENE

Hawk reaches the far side of the corral; makes a quick dash toward the gully.

THE GULLY

Red Bear spots Hawk, but is unable to get off a shot before the Cheyenne disappears into the gully.

Rifle ready, Red Bear waits to see if Hawk attacks.

ANNA

She hasn't moved from her place behind the well. She remains alert.

RANCH HOUSE ROOF

The Pawnee creeps to the top of the roof, moving closer to Anna.

THE GULLY

Red Bear, showing some anxiety, along with his hate for the Cheyenne, moves down the gully in Hawk's direction.

Several yards ahead, there is a bend in the ditch. Is Hawk just around that bend, waiting in ambush?

RANCH YARD

The Pawnee appears over the top of the roof; sees Anna. She remains unaware.

THE GULLY

Red Bear reaches the bend in the ditch. Hoping to surprise Hawk, he dives forward, landing on his belly and ready to fire at a concealed Hawk.

But, nobody is around that bend.

Momentarily bewildered, Red Bear HEARS a RIFLE COCK behind him. He spins around and sees:

RED BEAR'S P.O.V.

Hawk stands behind and above him on the edge of the gully, his rifle pointed directly at him.

RED BEAR

He is taken totally by surprise.

RED BEAR'S P.O.W.

Hawk FIRES the rifle.

INT. RANCH HOUSE. DAY.

With this last shot, Hanson is on his feet. He stumbles over to the kitchen area, where he finds a carving knife.

EXT. RANCH YARD. DAY.

The Pawnee moves further down the roof, preparing to shoot an arrow into Anna. His foot slips slightly.

Anna, crouching behind the well, HEARS the noise behind her. She turns; spots the Pawnee above her. Without a moment of hesitation, she FIRES her rifle.

The Pawnee is hit; falls head first off of the roof, landing almost on top of her.

HAWK

Having heard Anna's rifle fire, he rushes back toward the ranch house. Red Bear lies dead in the ditch.

BACK TO SCENE

Slightly in shock, Anna gives out a soft scream; pushes herself on the ground away from the dead Pawnee. She scrambles to her feet, turns and runs into:

HAWK

He catches her in his arms.

BACK TO SCENE

She gives out with a startled scream, then recognizes him. Still shaking, she holds onto him, tight. He does not object.

INT. RANCH HOUSE. DAY.

Knife in hand, Hanson reaches the door; opens it, and sees:

HANSON'S P.O.V.

Hawk's back is to him, partially concealing Anna. From his viewpoint, it appears as if the Cheyenne could be throttling her.

EXT. RANCH YARD. DAY.

Hanson lunges at Hawk with the knife.

> HANSON
> Don't hurt my Anna!

> ANNA
> (*Sees him coming*)
> No, Poppa!

Hawk spins around; grabs Hanson's arm as he starts to plunge the knife downward. The Cheyenne easily wrestles the weakened man to the ground.

> ANNA (*cont'd*)
> (*Going to her father; to Hawk*)
> He thought you were hurting me.

Hawk nods understanding.

> ANNA (*cont'd*)
> (*To Hanson*)
> It's all right, Poppa.

EXT. WOODED AREA. DAY.

Cochran, Bedford, Pugh and Bart rein their horses at the stream.
Running Wolf is bound to his horse, preventing his escape. As the
men water their horses; fill their canteens:

> COCHRAN
> Billy, me boy, who ever gave you the idea that you could
> follow a trail?

> BEDFORD
> You did.

> COCHRAN
> Well, I was mistaken.
> *(Takes a drink of water, then:)*
> I think we better change our strategy. Do some
> reconnoiterin'.

> BEDFORD
> How's that?

> COCHRAN
> Maybe we should split up. Each one of us go in a different
> direction. See what we can find.

> BEDFORD
> And, then?

> COCHRAN
> If one of us finds this Soarin' Hawk, follow 'im. Leave a
> trail that the rest of us can follow.

> PUGH
> How'll we know if one of us finds 'im if they don't come
> back and tell us?

COCHRAN
Good question, Brian. You're thinkin'.
(*Beat*)
Them of us that don't find 'im will meet back here at, say,
dusk. If somebody don't show up, then the rest of us'll just
head out in his direction and look for his trail.

BEDFORD
(*Indicating Running Wolf*)
What about the Injun?

COCHRAN
I'll keep the little bastard with me...in case I get lonely.

Cochran gives Bedford a lascivious wink.

EXT. RANCH YARD. DAY.

Hawk is behind the barn, digging a large hole in which to bury the
six dead Pawnee.

INT. RANCH HOUSE. DAY.

Hanson is propped up on his bed. drinking from a glass of water.
Anna sits on the edge of the bed.

HANSON
(Handing her the glass)
I feel better, now.

ANNA
Good, Poppa. You rest.

HANSON
Does he know?

ANNA
No. He does not know.
(*Beat*)
Poppa...where is Mama's trunk?

73

EXT. RANCH YARD. DAY.

Hawk is still digging the mass grave.

Anna, her hair down, comes out of the house wearing a long, very pretty dress. Somewhat apprehensive, she approaches Hawk, carrying a pitcher of water.

Hawk turns; sees her and his mouth drops, then widens into a broad grin of approval.

> HAWK
> Anna is very pretty in women's clothes.

> ANNA
> (*Blushes*)
> This was my mother's dress....I wanted you to see that I could dress like a woman.

> HAWK
> You will make a good wife.

Not quite knowing how to respond to that remark, she hands Hawk the pitcher. He nods thanks; drinks thirstily from it.

> ANNA
> (*Deliberately changing the subject*)
> I'd heard that Indians put their dead in trees...or someplace up high.

> HAWK
> (*Nods*)
> Cheyenne put dead in trees to help spirit rise to the Wise One Above. These Pawnee. They belong in ground.

> ANNA
> Oh.

> HAWK
> Anna and father no want dead Pawnee in trees if more Pawnee come.

                    ANNA
            (*Nods agreement; beat*)
    Where will you go when you leave here?

                    HAWK
    It is better that you not know.

He goes back to his digging.

                    ANNA
    Will you keep fighting the white man?

                    HAWK
    I will fight to protect my people.

                    ANNA
    What does that mean?

                    HAWK
    If Anna wants to be good wife, she should not ask so many
    questions. Go take care of father.

ATOP THE CLIFF

A tired Bedford rides up to the edge of the cliff above the ranch;
looks about and sees:

BEDFORD'S P.O.V.

Anna and Hawk are by the open mass grave that Hawk is digging.
She turns away; stomps back to the house. Hawk continues to dig.

ATOP THE CLIFF

                    BEDFORD
                (*To himself*)
        I'll be damned.

INT. RANCH HOUSE. DAY.

Anna comes in; notices that Hanson is staring at her. There are tears in his eyes.

ANNA
Poppa, what's wrong.

HANSON
You look just like your mother.

Anna goes to Hanson. They embrace.

EXT. RANCH YARD. DAY.

Hawk is continuing to dig the mass grave.

BEDFORD

He has worked his way down the cliff on the other side of the barn. Reaching the ground, he draws his revolver; presses himself against the barn and starts to move in Hawk's direction. As he rounds the corner of the structure:

BEDFORD'S P.O.V.

Hawk, his back to him, continues to dig.

BACK TO SCENE

Bedford moves forward; COCKS THE REVOLVER.

HAWK

He hears the sound.

BACK TO SCENE

Bedford takes another step forward.

> BEDFORD
>
> Hey, Injun. Turn around...slow.

Hawk doesn't move.

> BEDFORD (*cont'd*)
>
> Soars Like a Hawk, you hear me talkin' to you?

> HAWK
>
> I hear you.

Hawk suddenly spins around and flings a shovel full of dirt into Bedford's face.

Blinded, Bedford FIRES the revolver, but the shot goes wild.

Hawk dives into the man, knocking him to the ground. He pulls his knife; presses it against Bedford's throat.

> BEDFORD
>
> No...don't!

> HAWK
> (*Beat*)
>
> I know you....You killed my brothers.

> BEDFORD
>
> No....It weren't my idea.

> HAWK
>
> You killed my brothers!

He is about to slit Bedford's throat, when:

> ANNA (*O.S.*)
>
> No!

Hawk turns to see Anna standing at the corner of the barn, rifle in hand.

77

ANNA (*cont'd*)
Don't kill him.

HAWK
He is one of the men who killed my brothers.

ANNA
But, he's a white man.

Hawk reacts with hurt, contempt to her remark.

ANNA (*cont'd*)
(*Realizing her error*)
He should be turned over to the Army. They will punish him.

HAWK
They will give him a reward.

Once again, he gets ready to slit Bedford's throat.

BEDFORD
Wait!...We got one of yer "brothers"...the young 'un.

Hawk hesitates.

BEDFORD (*cont'd*)
The one you call Runnin' Wolf.

HAWK
Where is he?

BEDFORD
My friends got 'im....You might want to be tradin' me for him.

Hawk lowers the knife.

HAWK
(*To Anna*)

Get rope.

Anna nods; goes off to fetch the rope.

HAWK (*cont'd*)
(*To Bedford*)

Where your friends?

BEDFORD

Oh, I figure they'll be here sometime tomorrow mornin'.

HAWK
(*Beat*)

Good. Before I tie you up, you finish burying Pawnee. I tired.

BEDFORD

Go to hell, Injun.

HAWK

You want me shoot you in foot?

Bedford gives Hawk a nasty look, then starts to reach for the shovel.

HAWK (*cont'd*)

Use hands.

Bedford starts to object.

HAWK (*cont'd*)

Shoot foot.

Bedford mutters an obscenity, then he drops to his knees and begins to dig with his hands.

INT. RANCH HOUSE. DAY.

Hanson is propped up in his bed. Hawk, with rifle, enters, pushing a perspiration covered Bedford in front of him. Bedford's hands are bound behind his back. Anna, still carrying her rifle, is behind them; shuts the door.

> HAWK
> (*To Bedford; points to floor*)
> You stay there 'til morning.

Bedford sits; leans up against the wall.

> HANSON
> (*Frightened; confused*)
> What is this?

> ANNA
> This man, he....

> BEDFORD
> (*Recognizes Hanson; interrupts;*
> *friendly*)
> Oskar!

Hanson is speechless; Hawk and Anna, somewhat taken aback.

> BEDFORD (*cont'd*)
> I didn't know this were yer place.

> HAWK
> You know him?

> HANSON
> No, I....

> BEDFORD
> Sure, you know me, Oskar.
> (*Beat*)
> Didn't know yer daughter was sweet on an Injun.

HAWK
(*Kicks him*)
You keep mouth shut!

BEDFORD
Hey, why be mad at me? He was at Sand Creek, too.

Anna and Hanson both react with fear at Bedford's remark.

HAWK
(*Cocks rifle; to Bedford*)
You were at Sand Creek?

BEDFORD
Yeah, we had us a good old time that day.

Hawk raises the rifle to fire.

BEDFORD (*cont'd*)
If you want yer little brother back, you'd better not do that.

Hawk fights the desire to kill Bedford. Will he or won't he pull the trigger?

HAWK
Later I do that.

Suddenly, without warning, he smashes the man across the face with the rifle butt, knocking him out.

HAWK (*cont'd*)
(*Anger rising; to Hanson*)
You were at Sand Creek?

HANSON
(*Tears in his eyes*)
I...I...

> HAWK
> (*Raises his rifle*)
No need you for trade.

> ANNA

No!

Before Hawk can fire his weapon, Anna brings her rifle down hard onto the back of his head, knocking him out.

> BLACKOUT

FADE IN:

INT. RANCH HOUSE. DAY.

HAWK'S P.O.W: Lying on the floor, he opens his eyes to SEE Anna standing over him, holding the rifle.

A still somewhat anxious Hanson is propped up in the bed, watching him, while a sullen Bedford has regained consciousness; sits against the wall.

> ANNA
> (*To Hawk*)
Are you all right? Do you want some water?

Hawk shakes his head; starts to get up.

Anna levels the rifle at him.

> ANNA (*cont'd*)
You stay there!

Hawk remains in a sitting position.

> ANNA (*cont'd*)
My father wants to tell you something. You should listen to him.

                             HAWK
                            (*Beat*)
          I listen.

He turns to Hanson. After a long moment:

                            HANSON
          Indians have been stealing our horses...some cattle....I don't
          know what Indians...just Indians....Men come to our ranch,
          say they are going to get our horses back...that I should
          come with them to help....I take my Anna to Kirbytown,
          and I go with these men....Then there are more men...many
          men....We go to this place, Sand Creek....
                   (*Tears start to appear in his eyes*)
          All I wanted was my horses back.
                            (*Beat*)
          I did not know what those men would do....That they would
          kill....
                   (*Beat; recover himself*)
          I did not kill anyone that day. I did not hurt any one that
          day....

                             ANNA
          I told you. My father is a gentle man. He has never killed
          anybody.

Hawk studies Hanson for a long moment, then turns to Bedford, as if
to ask "Is he telling the truth?"

Bedford emits a nasty chuckle.

                           BEDFORD
                         (*With disdain*)
          The son-of-a-bitch is prob'ly tellin' the truth. He was
          throwin' up his guts out all over the place.

Hawk turns back toward Hanson for a moment, then:

>   HAWK
>   A good man does not follow his evil brothers.
>   (*To Anna; indicating Bedford*)
>   We must get ready for his friends.

Anna lowers the rifle. Hawk gets up; gets his rifle.

>   HAWK (*cont'd*)
>   (*To Anna: indicating Bedford*)
>   Watch him.

He exits the ranch house.

EXT. RANCH YARD. DAY.

Hawk heads for the back of the barn.

INT. RANCH HOUSE. DAY.

Anna, Hanson and Bedford are as we last saw them.

Hanson, with some difficulty, starts to get up out of bed.

>   ANNA
>   (*With concern*)
>   Papa....

>   HANSON
>   I'm hungry.

>   ANNA
>   Stay there. I'll get you something.

>   HANSON
>   I get it.

On his feet, he heads for the kitchen area.

>   BEDFORD
>   (*Starts to get up; indicating Hawk*)
>   He's gone. Cut me loose.

ANNA
(*Points rifle at him*)
Be quiet.

As Hanson passes by Bedford:

BEDFORD
Hey, he's an Injun. I'm white.

Suddenly, Hanson kicks Bedford in the face, knocking him down onto the floor. Hanson grabs the table to retain his balance.

HANSON
My daughter say, "Be quiet".

He continues to the kitchen area.

EXT. ATOP THE CLIFF. DAY.

Hawk finishes scaling the cliff above the Hanson ranch. He spots Bedford's horse (a Bay), tied to a tree; mounts it and rides it around and down a gradual slope that leads to the front part of the ranch.

EXT. RANCH YARD. DAY.

Hawk has removed the saddle from Bedford's horse and put the animal in the corral. He also carries Bedford's rifle, as well as his own.

Anna comes out of the house; goes to him.

ANNA
Can I help?

HAWK
(*Nods*)
White man?

ANNA
Poppa's watching him.

INT. RANCH HOUSE. DAY.

Bedford is still on the floor. Hanson sits in a chair at the table, drinking coffee. The rifle is across his lap.

> BEDFORD
> They're gonna hang you as a renegade, Oskar.

> HANSON
> Good coffee.

He takes another sip.

EXT. RANCH YARD. DAY.

Hawk and Anna are as we last saw them.

> HAWK
> Help with buckboard.

They go to the buckboard. During the following, they push it into a position so that it can better serve as cover.

> ANNA
> I'm sorry I hit you.

> HAWK
> You were protecting father.
> (*Rubs back of head*)
> Glad you not angry at me.

> ANNA
> This Running Wolf....He's your brother?

> HAWK
> All Cheyenne are my brothers.... Running Wolf is young brave who wishes to be warrior. Maybe wishes too much.

> ANNA
> You care about him.

                    HAWK
       I care.

The buckboard in place, Hawk heads back toward the house.

                    HAWK (*cont'd*)
       Now we check rifles.

EXT. HANSON RANCH HOUSE. NIGHT.

A single lamp is lit inside.

INT. RANCH HOUSE. NIGHT.

Hawk, Anna and Hanson are checking, loading their respective
rifles. A dour Bedford sits on the floor, watching them.

Hawk finishes with his weapon.

                    HAWK
       I go, get ready, now.

He exits. Anna goes after him.

EXT. HANSON RANCH HOUSE. NIGHT.

Hawk comes out of the house; looks up at the cliff. Anna is right
behind him; shuts the door after her.

                    ANNA
       What are you going to do?

                    HAWK
       Not good that our enemy is above us. I climb up there.
       Wait for them.

                    ANNA
       You...You'll be outnumbered.

HAWK
(*Starts for the cliff*)
Maybe I surprise them.

ANNA
Wait!...What if we could get them to come down here?

HAWK
That would be good...but how we do that?

ANNA
Maybe I could do that.

Hawk looks at her, not quite sure what she's up to.

EXT. THE PRAIRIE. DAY.

Cochran, Pugh, Bart and Running Wolf, tied to his horse, ride along slowly, following Bedford's trail.

RUNNING WOLF

He is seething with anger; ready to explode.

BACK TO SCENE

BART
(*To Cochran*)
You sure we're goin' the right way?

COCHRAN
(*Nods; points to marker*)
Billy Ray can't follow a trail, but he sure knows how to mark one.

PUGH
What d'ya think happened to him?

COCHRAN
If I knew that, Brian, me lad, I'd be a fortune teller.

EXT. RANCH YARD. DAY.

Anna, in a skirt, apron and blouse that reveals her bare arms, has hung up a clothesline and is doing some washing in a tub. She appears oblivious to any threat.

EXT. ATOP THE CLIFF. DAY.

Cochran, Pugh, Bart and Running Wolf arrive at the cliff that overlooks the Hanson ranch. Cochran peers down and sees:

COCHRAN'S P.O.V.

Anna is doing her washing; hanging clothing and sheets onto the clothesline.

BACK TO SCENE

> COCHRAN
> Well, what do we have here?

> PUGH
> It's a ranch.

> COCHRAN
> Thank you, Brian.

He continues to look over the ranch, and he sees:

COCHRAN'S P.O.V.

The corral, which among other horses, holds Bedford's Bay.

BACK TO SCENE

> COCHRAN
> Billy Ray's here alright.

> PUGH
> How do you know?

COCHRAN

That's his Bay in the corral.

PUGH

Where is he?

COCHRAN

Probably inside the house....Looks like he found himself some female company.

He kicks his horse, leading the group around and down to the slope that goes to the ranch.

COCHRAN (*cont'd*)

I just hope he plans to share it.

EXT. RANCH YARD. DAY.

As Cochran and company make their way down the slope behind her, Anna is definitely aware of their presence, but she does not let on.

COCHRAN AND COMPANY

They reach the bottom of the slope; head toward the ranch entrance. As they approach, Cochran looks about. A sixth sense tells him that something is not quite right.

COCHRAN

(*To Pugh and Bart*)

You boys hang back a bit. I'll go in an' have a look see.

(*Beat*)

Watch the Injun.

Leaving the others behind, he rides into the ranch yard.

BACK TO SCENE

Anna is briefly disturbed that Cochran has come into the yard alone. She momentarily rests her hand on the butt of Bedford's revolver that is hidden beneath her apron; hides her concern with a welcoming smile.

> ANNA
>
> Good morning, sir.

> COCHRAN
>
> 'Morning to you, ma'm. And how are you on this fine day?

> ANNA
>
> Just fine.

THE GULLY

Hawk, rifle ready, lies on his stomach, waiting for the right moment to make his move.

Unfortunately, Bart and Pugh are positioned just in front and above him, so that he is unable to get off a shot without first revealing his position.

BACK TO SCENE

> ANNA
> (*Indicating well*)
> Would you and your friends like to fill your canteens?

> COCHRAN
>
> That's very kind of you, ma'm. Thank you.

> ANNA
>
> Have your friends come in.

> COCHRAN
>
> Actually, ma'm, I wanted to ask you about that Bay in yer corral there. Looks like one that belongs to a mate o' mine.

> ANNA
>
> Oh, do you know Mr. Bedford?

                    COCHRAN
        Billy Ray and me are like brothers.

                     ANNA
        He's inside eating his breakfast.

INT. RANCH HOUSE. DAY.

Bedford is on the floor, hands tied behind his back, a gag in his mouth.

An anxious Hanson is by the window, rifle in hand.

                   ANNA (*O.S.*)
                  (*Continuing*)
        Would you like to join him?

EXT. RANCH YARD. DAY.

Cochran considers Anna's offer for a moment, then:

                    COCHRAN
        Why don't you ask him to step out here?

ANNA

She reaches down; again touches the revolver beneath her apron.

COCHRAN

He notes her move, and:

BACK TO SCENE

In one swift move, Cochran draws, cocks and points his revolver directly at Anna's chest.

                    COCHRAN
        Don't make me shoot you, ma'm. It'd be such a waste.

INT. RANCH HOUSE. DAY.

Hanson blanches at the sight of his daughter in danger.

> HANSON
> (*To himself*)
> Anna....

BEDFORD

With Hanson's attention elsewhere, he is trying to work his tied hands free, rubbing them against a nail in the wall.

EXT. RANCH YARD. DAY.

> COCHRAN
> (*Calls toward house*)
> Billy Ray! Get your bloody ass out here!
> (*To Anna*)
> Beggin' yer pardon, ma'm.

THE GULLY

Though he can't see the ranch yard from his position, Hawk knows that something is wrong and that he must make a move.

He jumps to his feet; aims his rifle.

BART

He spots Hawk.

> BART
> (*Shouts*)
> It's an ambush!

COCHRAN

He turns his attention toward Bart.

HAWK

He FIRES his rifle.

BART

He's hit in the chest; falls dead.

PUGH

He spots Hawk; draws and FIRES his pistol at him.

HAWK

The shot misses him.

RUNNING WOLF

He tries to slip off his horse, but:

PUGH

                    PUGH
        Stay put, Injun!

He hits the young Cheyenne across the back of the head with his revolver, knocking him onto the ground.

HAWK

He FIRES at Pugh; misses.

INT. RANCH HOUSE. DAY.

Hanson FIRES his rifle through the window.

EXT. RANCH YARD. DAY.

The bullet strikes the side of the well; ricochets harmlessly away.

Anna draws her revolver; FIRES it at Cochran. She misses.

Cochran's horse rears up, but he controls it.

COCHRAN
(*To Anna; indicating Hawk*)
'Scuse me, ma'm. He's the one I want.

He rides toward Hawk; FIRING his pistol as he goes.

COCHRAN AND PUGH

They both ride toward Hawk, FIRING their pistols.

HAWK

He dives for cover back into the gully.

INT. RANCH HOUSE. DAY.

His hands now untied, Bedford rushes Hanson; grabs the rifle and hits him across the face with the butt, knocking him to the ground.

BEDFORD
(*Pointing the rifle at him*)
I oughta kill you right now, you son-of-a-bitch!

Instead, he turns his attention to the front door.

EXT. THE GULLY. DAY.

Hawk races down the ravine, with Cochran and Pugh chasing him on horseback.

EXT. RANCH YARD. DAY.

Anna, revolver in hand, has run to the entrance of the ranch yard to watch Cochran and Pugh's pursuit of Hawk. She wants to help the Cheyenne, but doesn't quite know how.

Bedford emerges from the house, rifle in hand, and, without her being aware of him, hurries up behind Anna.

Bedford grabs Anna from behind; wrestles her to the ground and disarms her.

THE GULLY

Cochran and Pugh are almost upon Hawk when the Cheyenne suddenly spins; FIRES his rifle.

PUGH

He's hit point blank; falls off his horse, dead.

COCHRAN

He momentarily reacts to his companion's demise.

HAWK

He seizes the opportunity to rush up the side of the gully; leap up at Cochran and knock him off his horse. The two men go sprawling.

HAWK AND COCHRAN

The two men struggle. Hawk, knife in his hand and hate in his eyes, is out for blood. Cochran was, after all, the leader of the ambush.

As the Cheyenne is getting the best of the Irishman and is about to plunge the knife into his chest:

TWO SHOTS O.S.

Hawk looks up and sees:

HAWK'S P.O.V.

In the ranch yard, Bedford is holding Anna. One arm is wrapped around her neck and the other is holding a six-gun to her temple.

                    BEDFORD
                    (*Shouts*)
          Give it up, Injun!

HAWK

He's torn. He wants to kill Cochran more than anything, but Anna is being threatened.

He raises his arm, ready to finish Cochran, then suddenly drops his hand to his side; a sign of surrender. He does not release the knife, but, unseen by Cochran, slips it into its sheath.

HAWK AND COCHRAN

Cochran gets to his feet; glowers silently at Hawk, looks down at Pugh's corpse, then back at the Cheyenne.

HAWK
(*To Cochran*)
You no hurt Anna or her father.

COCHRAN
(*Picking up his hat and revolver*)
I don't give a bloody damn about them...
(*Indicating Running Wolf*)
...or yer little friend over there.

He points his revolver at Hawk.

COCHRAN
(*continuing*)
Yer the one I want. You're a right valuable Injun. Worth a thousand dollars...dead or alive.
(*Indicating Anna*)
Unfortunately, I can't shoot you down in front of no witness.

HAWK
(*Indicating Bedford*)
Tell him let her go. Then, I go with you.

Cochran ponders a moment, then:

97

COCHRAN

Sure.

(*Calls to Bedford*)
Let go of her, Billy Ray...but watch her.

ANNA AND BEDFORD

Bedford lowers the revolver and releases his grip on Anna's neck, but keeps her next to him.

HAWK AND COCHRAN

COCHRAN
(*Grabs the reins of his horse;
motions to Hawk*)
Let's join 'em.

They walk back toward the ranch yard. Cochran leads his horse with one hand; covers Hawk with the revolver with his other.

COCHRAN (*cont'd*)
(*Indicating Pugh*)
Too bad about Brian there. He was a good lad. Gonna miss him.
(*Beat*)
Too bad about the lady and her father there, too.
HAWK
Why too bad about them?

COCHRAN

Hell, after the folks in town hear they were helpin' a renegade Injun...they'll be lucky if they just get burned out.

HAWK

Then they no hear that.

Without warning, Hawk spins around and plunges his knife into Cochran's heart.

Total shock and surprise on the Irishman's face, as blood spurts out of his mouth and he collapses to the ground, dead.

BEDFORD

He panics; FIRES a wild shot in Hawk's direction.

ANNA

She backs away; heads for the house.

HAWK

He grabs Cochran's revolver; jumps onto his horse and gallops toward Bedford.

BEDFORD

Realizing he is alone, he FIRES another wild shot at Hawk; turns and starts to run, trying to catch Anna.

HAWK

He bears down on Bedford; FIRES several shots at him.

BEDFORD

He is about to grab Anna when he is hit by Hawk's bullet. He falls to the ground.

BACK TO SCENE

With Anna watching from the porch, Hawk jumps off the horse; races over to the downed Bedford. Knife in hand, he leaps onto the man; savagely plunges the blade into him.

ANNA

She's shocked by his fury.

BACK TO SCENE

Exhausted, Hawk looks at Anna; their eyes fixed on each other for a long wordless moment that says, "It's over". Finally:

> HAWK
>
> Father?

> ANNA
> (*Shakes head*)
>
> I'll see.

> HAWK
> (*Getting up*)
>
> I see to Running Wolf.

INT. RANCH HOUSE. DAY.

Hanson is on the floor, attempting to get up, as Anna rushes inside.

> ANNA
> (*Going to him*)
>
> Poppa!

As she helps him up:

> HANSON
>
> I am not hurt.

EXT. OUTSIDE THE RANCH YARD. DAY.

Hands tied behind his back, Running Wolf is still on the ground, attempting to get up. He is dazed, confused, frustrated, angry.

Hawk hurries over to him, and as he unties the young Cheyenne:

> HAWK
> "Are you all right, little brother?"

> RUNNING WOLF
> "I am not worthy to be a Cheyenne."

                    HAWK
"Why do you speak this way? I have seen your bravery.
Someday you will be a great warrior."

                RUNNING WOLF
"I allowed those men to capture me. To bring disgrace
upon me."

                    HAWK
"It could not be helped. There is no shame in that."

                RUNNING WOLF
"Those men were at Sand Creek."

                    HAWK
"And, now they are dead. It is over."

He helps Running Wolf to his feet.

                HAWK (*cont'd*)
"Not all whites are bad. Come, I show you."

They start walking back toward the ranch yard.

EXT. RANCH YARD. DAY.

Anna and Hanson emerge from the house. He sits down on the
porch steps, as Anna goes over and retrieves the revolver next to
Bedford's body; puts it into her apron pocket.

Hawk and Running Wolf enter the ranch yard; head toward the
house.

ANNA

She sees the two Cheyenne; smiles and starts toward them.

HAWK

More relaxed, his attention is on Anna.

RUNNING WOLF

His eyes focus on the porch.

RUNNING WOLF'S P.O.V.

An exhausted Hanson sits on the porch, casually looking in his direction.

RUNNING WOLF

He remembers:

EXT. CHEYENNE CAMP. DAY.

FLASHBACK SEQUENCE: Hanson rides into the camp; reins his horse. He has yet to fire his weapon; is totally shocked by the slaughter going on around him.

RUNNING WOLF

The young, frightened brave, knife in hand, is crouched against the side of a teepee, not quite sure what to do. Then, he spots Hanson, who seems to be in a like quandary, and he makes a decision.

BACK TO SCENE

Running Wolf, knife in hand, runs out from his hiding place; leaps up at Hanson, knocking him off his horse. The two men go sprawling onto the ground, and with the Cheyenne on top, they struggle for the knife. END FLASHBACK SEQUENCE.

EXT. RANCH YARD. DAY.

A sudden fury overtakes Running Wolf.

                    RUNNING WOLF
                      (*Shouts*)
        "Sand Creek!"

He snatches the knife from the sheath on Hawk's belt and races toward Hanson, ready to strike.

RUNNING WOLF'S P.O.V.

He bears down on a frightened Hanson.

HAWK

                    HAWK
              (*Taken aback; shouts:*)
     "No!"

He starts after Running Wolf.

ANNA

She's startled, as Running Wolf rushes past her.

HANSON

He tries to get up; stumbles backwards.

RUNNING WOLF

He is almost upon Hanson. He leaps at him for the kill.

O.S. GUNSHOT.

Running Wolf falls dead.

HAWK

He stops, in shock; looks toward:

ANNA

She holds a smoking revolver.

ANNA
(Tearful; to Hawk)
My father....

HAWK

Frustrated, angry, he masks his feelings; turns and walks away.

BACK TO SCENE

Anna watches Hawk walk out of the ranch yard, then she turns and looks at Hanson, their faces expressing the tragedy of what has just happened.

DISSOLVE TO:

EXT. RANCH YARD. DAY.

Later that day. Hawk has two of Cochran's horses. He ties Running Wolf's body, wrapped in cloth, across the back of one of the animals.

Anna watches from the porch, hesitant to approach him.

Hawk goes to the other horse; checks his retrieved Henry rifle. He is about to mount the animal, then turns; looks at Anna. Leading the two horses, he walks over to her.

HAWK
I do not hate you, Anna. I know that you are sorry.

Anna is too choked up with tears to speak. She can only nod.

HAWK *(cont'd)*
You are a good woman.
(He mounts his horse)
You find good man.

With that, he kicks his horse; rides out of the ranch yard.

Hanson comes out of the house; stands next to his daughter, as they watch the two horses disappear into the distance.

DISSOLVE TO:

EXT. OUTSIDE THE RANCH YARD. DUSK.

The bodies of Cochran and his men are still lying about, as Lieutenant Hall, Sergeant Bates and the four troopers ride into the yard.

EXT. RANCH YARD. DUSK.

Anna, wearing a dress, emerges from the house, followed by Hanson. Lieutenant Hall rides over to them.

> LT. HALL
> (*Taken aback*)

Miss Hanson....

> ANNA

Lieutenant....

> LT. HALL

What happened here?

> ANNA

These men. They tried to steal our horses. We kill them.

> LT. HALL

You and your father did all this?

> ANNA

We did.

> LT. HALL
> (*Impressed*)

Are you all right?

ANNA
We will be fine...but if you would take these men away....

LT. HALL
Certainly. We'll do that.
(*Beat*)
You look very pretty in a dress, m'am.

ANNA
(*Blushes*)
Thank you, Lieutenant.

LT. HALL
I keep askin' and you don't give be an answer, but there's another dance at the fort this Saturday, and I'd be mighty proud if you'd let me escort you.

Anna hesitates; looks at Hanson. He nods his approval.

ANNA
I would like to go, Lieutenant.

LT. HALL
(*Beams a smile*)
That's just great, ma"m.

She smiles back at him.

DISSOLVE TO:

EXT. MOUNTAIN TRAIL. DUSK.

Hawk has finished placing Running Wolf's wrapped body high in a tree.

HAWK
"Sleep well, little brother."

He mounts his horse, and as he proceeds down the trail into the sunset:

WHITE BULL (*V.O.*)
Your journey will be long. You will lead our people in
battle against the Pawnee...whites...other enemies, but you
will also help to forge a bridge of peace.

Hawk disappears down the trail.

FADE OUT.

THE END

Michael B. Druxman

"HAWK"

EXT. FOREST CLEARING. DAY.

A clearing in a wooded area, somewhere in the Rocky Mountains. Patches of snow are on the ground. UNDER THE CREDITS, we survey this peaceful, untouched setting, ultimately focusing on a rabbit seeking food.

WHITE TRAPPER

A WHITE TRAPPER, 30s, bearded, hungry and dressed for the cold is on the other side of the clearing. His horse and pack mule are tied to a tree behind him. He raises his single shot rifle; aims at the small animal and FIRES.

His pleased expression tells us that he has killed his dinner. He hurries across the clearing to claim his prize. As he picks up the dead rabbit, he senses something. His attention goes toward the trees.

WHITE TRAPPER'S P.O.V.

There is no movement in the trees, just a distant O.S. RUMBLE.

BACK TO SCENE

The Trapper listens, as the rumble becomes LOUDER, like the SOUND OF APPROACHING HORSES.

He blanches, then with rabbit and rifle in hand, he starts to back toward the other side of the clearing. Suddenly, he sees:

WHITE TRAPPER'S P.O.V.

A Cheyenne hunting party, consisting of three braves on horseback, gallops out from the trees. They are: TALL ELK (30s), a pragmatic warrior with a stately bearing, CRAZY BUFFALO (late 20s), tall, muscular and sullen, and YELLOW MOCCASIN (30s), who listens more than he talks. They are armed with bow and arrows and single shot rifles.

BACK TO SCENE

The Trapper panics; turns and makes a dash for his horses on the other side of the clearing. The Cheyenne gallop after him; surround him in the middle of the clearing. Frightened, the Trapper drops his rifle. Still holding the rabbit, he raises his hands in surrender. Crazy Buffalo takes his bow and arrow; aims it at the Trapper.

> TRAPPER
> (*Pleading*)

I was hungry.

> CRAZY BUFFALO

You are hunting on Cheyenne land.

He pulls back the drawstring of his bow.

> TRAPPER

No...!

> HAWK (*O.S.*)
> (*Calls*)

Crazy Buffalo!

Everybody's attention goes toward:

SOARS LIKE A HAWK

He has emerged from the trees, riding a Pinto; heads toward the group. SOARS LIKE A HAWK (30s) is a handsome gallant warrior with strong, classic features. A charismatic, levelheaded leader, Hawk is in line to become a Council chief. He carries a Henry rifle. As he reaches his fellow Cheyenne, he shakes his head.

HAWK
(*To Crazy Buffalo*)
If you kill this white man, the soldiers will come. They will attack our people.

BACK TO SCENE

HAWK
(*Continuing*)
Crazy Buffalo, it is only a rabbit.

CRAZY BUFFALO
It is a Cheyenne rabbit.

HAWK
The Pawnee come on our land. Maybe their rabbits come here, too.

He indicates that the Trapper should hand him the rabbit. The Trapper willingly complies.

CRAZY BUFFALO
Soars Like a Hawk talks like his white friends. He sounds like a woman.

HAWK
(*Looks at rabbit*)
No, I think this is a Pawnee rabbit.
(*Tosses rabbit back to the Trapper*)
Eat it, white man. Get a belly ache.

As Tall Elk and Yellow Moccasin chuckle at Hawk's joke, Crazy Buffalo grunts; gallops off. Tall Elk and Yellow Moccasin follow.

The Trapper nods a grateful "thank you" to Hawk, who responds with an expression that says, "You'd better get out of here while the getting is good," then he rides off after his fellow braves.

The Trapper snatches up his rifle; hurries over to his horses.

EXT. MOUNTAIN TRAIL. DAY.

CREDITS CONCLUDE, as the four Cheyenne make their way along the ridge. They have two pack horses, one of which has a dead elk strapped across its back.

EXT. CHEYENNE CAMP. DAY.

A Cheyenne winter camp. Patches of snow are on the ground. Dozens of teepees are clustered together at a horseshoe bend of the shallow creek. Horses are tethered away from the teepees. Cheyenne men, women and children peacefully go about their daily chores.

Among them are WHITE ANTELOPE (40), one of the chiefs, RUNNING WOLF (17), a young brave, eager to prove himself, who is working on his bow, and LITTLE BUTTERFLY (18), an attractive Cheyenne maiden, soon to be Hawk's bride. She is carrying a jug of water toward one of the teepees.

TITLE CARD: "Sand Creek, Colorado Territory, November 29, 1864"

White Antelope, who has been talking with a Cheyenne Brave, glances off, and sees:

WHITE ANTELOPE'S P.O.V.

A troop of several hundred Militia, both in uniform and civilian clothing, are taking their positions along the ridge of the hill above the camp. Cannons are being made ready to fire.

BACK TO SCENE

All of the Cheyenne appear anxious, confused.

Little Butterfly gasps in fear; drops her jug. It smashes onto the ground.

Women and children run to their teepees.

ATOP THE RIDGE

The Militia continues its preparations for the attack.

Leader of the force is COLONEL JOHN M. CHIVINGTON (43), tall, burly, bearded; dressed in full uniform. A Methodist minister, he has been described as "a crazy preacher who thinks he's Napoleon Bonaparte". Surrounding him are five scruffy opportunistic drifters in civilian clothes, none of whom you would ever invite to your home for dinner.

They are JAMES COCHRAN (late 30s), an Irish immigrant/buffalo hunter, BILLY RAY BEDFORD (30s), a Confederate Army deserter from Alabama and BRIAN PUGH (20s), a young man with a slight build and the mentality of a child, who does Cochran's every bidding. Additionally, FRANK and BART, both in their 20s.

Also among the Militia is Swedish immigrant/small rancher OSKAR HANSON (30), a strong, but gentle man who feels uncomfortable in his present company.

ROSE CARMICHAEL (mid-20s), a half-Irish/half-Cheyenne Army scout, rides over to Chivington. If she had half-a-mind to do something about it, Rose could be a very attractive woman, but since she has never had a female role model, she prefers the company of men. She dresses like a man, swears like a man, drinks like a man and, when she's in a saloon, claims that she can "lick any man in the house". That's why she's garnered the nickname, "Rowdy Rose". A realist, Rose would prefer to ignore her Native American heritage, since she knows that her future lies with the Whites.

> ROSE
> I know them Cheyenne down there, Colonel. They're peaceable. No need to attack.

> CHIVINGTON
> They're hostiles, Miss Carmichael, and I intend to do God's work.

ROSE
There're women and children down there.

CHIVINGTON
And they've been harboring the hostiles that have been raiding our ranches.

ROSE
They're under the Army's protection.

CHIVINGTON
I told the General he shouldn't send you....Woman, I am the leader of this expedition. You are an Army scout assigned to me. You will follow my orders.
(*Beat*)
Mr. Cochran, if this "woman" tries to interfere, shoot her.

COCHRAN
(*Irish accent*)
Yes, Colonel, sir.

Cochran, Bedford and Pugh draw their weapons; point them at Rose.

COCHRAN (*cont'd*)
(*To Pugh*)
Such a shame to kill a lady.

PUGH
You call that half-breed a lady?

COCHRAN
(*Shrugs*)
Out here, my boy, you take what you can get.

Rose throws Cochran a nasty look, but her attention is drawn to:

CHEYENNE CAMP

White Antelope, wearing a headdress, emerges from a teepee, carrying an American flag. He mounts his horse; turns to the anxious Cheyenne, including Running Wolf and Little Butterfly, who surround him.

> WHITE ANTELOPE
> They will see their flag and know we wish to live with them in peace.

He rides out toward the ridge.

ATOP THE RIDGE

Chivington, Rose and others watch White Antelope ride in their direction.

> ROSE
> See, Colonel! That's White Antelope. He's no hostile. He's carryin' an American flag.

> CHIVINGTON
> (*Ignoring her; calls:*)
> Prepare to fire!

The cannon crew gets ready to fire its weapon.

> ROSE
> You son-of-a-bitch!

> BEDFORD
> Colonel told ya to shut up!

Bedford hits Rose across the back of the head with the butt of his revolver. She falls off her horse, unconscious.

> CHIVINGTON
> (*Raises arm; to cannon crew*)
> Fire!

The cannon FIRES.

CHEYENNE CAMP

The cannon ball explodes several feet away from White Antelope. Furious, the Cheyenne chief tosses the flag onto the ground.

Behind him, Little Butterfly and the other women watch, terrified. Running Wolf and the other men grab their old rifles, bows and other inadequate weapons.

ATOP THE RIDGE

> CHIVINGTON
> (*Calls out*)
> No quarter, gentlemen! Charge!

His saber high, Chivington spurs his horse, leads his men in a charge down the hill toward the Cheyenne camp. The large contingent of men follow, FIRING at will.

Hanson, reluctantly, rides with the troop, but he does not fire his weapon.

Cochran, Bedford, Pugh, Frank and Bart race their mounts down the hill, firing their weapons, having a good ol' time.

WHITE ANTELOPE

He is struck in the chest by two bullets; falls off of his horse, dead.

THE FLAG

Chivington's troops ride over the American flag, trampling it into the dust.

CHEYENNE CAMP

As the Militia rides into the camp, firing their weapons, screaming women and children run for cover.

Cheyenne braves put up a futile attempt to protect their camp, but are cut down by the overwhelming force.

Cheyenne men, women and children are shot down without mercy.

One woman is stripped naked, raped, then stabbed to death.

Militia members set fire to the teepees.

ATOP THE RIDGE

A dazed Rose pushes herself up from the ground; watches the massacre, unable to help. Then, she collapses again.

CHEYENNE CAMP

Pugh rides into the camp; FIRES his weapon.

RUNNING WOLF

The young, frightened brave, knife in hand, is crouched against the side of a teepee, not quite sure what to do. Then, he spots Pugh.

BACK TO SCENE

Running Wolf, knife in hand, runs out from his hiding place; leaps up at Pugh, knocking him off his horse. The two men go sprawling onto the ground, and with the Cheyenne on top, they struggle for the knife. Pugh is definitely losing.

COCHRAN

He rides up; spots Running Wolf on top of Pugh and FIRES his revolver.

BACK TO SCENE

The bullet hits Running Wolf in the back. The dead Cheyenne falls off of Pugh, who scrambles to his feet; retrieves his gun and starts FIRING again.

Cochran also rides off to do some more killing.

HANSON

He rides into the camp; reins his horse. He has yet to fire his weapon; is totally shocked by the slaughter going on around him. After a moment, he jumps off of his horse; throws up onto the ground.

A RAVINE

A group of Cheyenne women and children huddle in fear in the rock-filled quarry.

Troopers spot them, FIRE their weapons down at them. Bedford and Cochran are among this group.

THE CAMP

Little Butterfly dashes out from inside a teepee, runs toward a wooded area, then turns and sees:

LITTLE BUTTERFLY'S P.O.V.

TROOPER JONES (late 20s), saber raised, is riding directly at her.

BACK TO SCENE

Little Butterfly is frozen in her tracks. Trooper Jones rides by, beheading her with his saber.

BLACKOUT

EXT. FOREST CLEARING. DAY.

Hawk and the rest of the hunting party emerge from the wooded area; move across the clearing. Crazy Buffalo is riding point.

Hawk's mind appears to be elsewhere, as Tall Elk rides up next to him.

TALL ELK

Soars Like a Hawk's thoughts are not here. Are they with Little Butterfly?

Hawk doesn't answer; just smiles.

TALL ELK (*cont'd*)

She will make you a good wife... even if Crazy Buffalo is her brother.

HAWK

Crazy Buffalo will not be living in our teepee.

CRAZY BUFFALO

He spots something up ahead.

CRAZY BUFFALO'S P.O.V.

In the distance, across the creek, SMOKE is rising from the Cheyenne camp.

BACK TO SCENE

CRAZY BUFFALO
(*Calls to Hawk, etal.*)

There is trouble!

Hawk and the others see the smoke.

HAWK
(*Blanches*)

Little Butterfly....

He kicks his horse; races ahead of the others toward the camp.

Crazy Buffalo and the others follow quickly behind him.

EXT. CHEYENNE CAMP. DAY.

Hawk rides into the camp; reins his horse and dismounts, when he sees:

HAWK'S P.O.V.

Total devastation. Dead and dismembered bodies are everywhere. All the teepees have been burned to the ground. There are only a few survivors, and they are not in the best of shape.

BACK TO SCENE

> HAWK
> (*Screams*)
> Little Butterfly!

As Crazy Buffalo and the others arrive on the scene, also reacting with shock and anger, Hawk rushes through the camp, searching. He stops when he sees:

HAWK'S P.O.V.

Corpses of the women and children who were shot down in the ravine.

BACK TO SCENE

Moving more slowly, almost in a daze, Hawk walks through the camp, viewing the ruin. He stops when he sees:

HAWK'S P.O.V.

What is apparently the beheaded body of Little Butterfly.

BACK TO SCENE

There are tears behind Hawk's eyes, but they will not come. He drops to his knees; begins to sing the Cheyenne funeral chant.

Crazy Buffalo and the other members of the hunting party, all feeling various degrees of anguish, approach Hawk, but maintain a discreet distance.

EXT. KIRBYTOWN. NIGHT.

Stuck out in the middle of a plain, this is not really a town, but more of an extended trading post that services the nearby fort, travelers, plus ranches and farms in the area.

On a muddy "street," one long frame building with a wooden sidewalk in front of it houses a general store, saloon/cafe and small hotel. A sign along the building top, reads "Kirby's". Several horses are tied to the hitching post in front.

AMOS DRUCKER (late 40s), a crusty, veteran Army scout of mixed parentage, rides into town and over to the saloon where he dismounts.

INT. SALOON. NIGHT.

Nothing fancy. There's a bar, several tables; stairs leading upward to a second floor. Bedford, Bart, Frank and several other members of Chivington's Militia are at the bar, drinking, laughing; celebrating their victory. ED KIRBY (50s), the owner of most of the town, is behind the bar, serving them drinks.

BEDFORD
(Half-drunk; Bragging to Kirby)

Chivington showed them Injuns, all right. He put the fear of God in 'em.

BART

That he did.

BEDFORD

He's gonna get himself elected to Congress yet.

ROSE (*O.S.*)
(*Calls*)

Ed!

ROSE

She sits alone at a corner table, a glass and whiskey bottle in front of her. Brooding, she's had far too much to drink.

BACK TO SCENE

Ed looks in her direction.

ROSE
Bring me another bottle.

Bedford gives Bart and Frank a lecherous wink. He takes a whiskey bottle from the bar; walks over to Rose's table.

BEDFORD
Hey, Rose, let me buy you a drink.

ROSE
Don't want yer goddamn drink.

BEDFORD
Forget about today. Why don't we let bygones be bygones? Go upstairs and have some fun.

ROSE
Why don't you kiss my sweaty ass?

BEDFORD
Bitch!

He starts back to the bar, then:

BEDFORD (*cont'd*)
(*To Rose*)
By the way, how's yer head?

He emits a nasty chuckle; turns from her:

                    ROSE
        Just fine.

She snatches up the empty whiskey bottle from her table, smashes it across the back of his head.

                    ROSE (*cont'd*)
        How's yours?

Bedford falls to the floor, unconscious.

FRANK AND BART

Startled, they reach for their revolvers.

                    DRUCKER (*O.S.*)
        Hold it!

The two men turn to see:

DRUCKER

He has his revolver out, pointed at them.

                    DRUCKER
        Just keep 'em holstered, boys.

BACK TO SCENE

Frank and Bart know Drucker and don't want to fight him. They turn back to their drinks.

                    DRUCKER
                (*Nods to Kirby*)
        Ed....

Ed gives him a nod of approval. Drucker looks over at Rose.

DRUCKER (*cont'd*)
Hello, Rose.

ROSE
What're you doin' here, Amos?

DRUCKER
The General's lookin' for ya.

ROSE
He's lookin' for me?

DRUCKER
You didn't report.

ROSE
Report what?...Our great victory?

DRUCKER
(*Goes to her*)
Let's go outside. Get you some fresh air.

ROSE
(*Beat*)
Good idea.

She allows him to take her arm. As they start out, Bedford raises his head, moans.

ROSE (*cont'd*)
(*To Bedford*)
Didn't ask you, asshole!

She kicks him in the head, knocking him out. As Drucker leads her out:

ROSE (*cont'd*)
(*Calls back to Bedford*)
Keep yer goddamn mouth shut, next time.

EXT. KIRBYTOWN. NIGHT.

The street is empty. Drucker and Rose emerge from the saloon. He escorts her toward their horses.

> ### DRUCKER
> You need some coffee in you before you see the General.

> ### ROSE
> I don't want to see no goddamn General.

> ### DRUCKER
> (*Beat*)
> What happened out there, Rose?

> ### ROSE
> (*Beat*)
> Amos, you taught me damn good. You taught me how to track....You taught me how to fight....You taught me how to kill....Hell, I'm almost as good a scout as you.

> ### DRUCKER
> Almost.

> ### ROSE
> But, one thing you didn't teach me....You didn't teach me how to stop it.

> ### DRUCKER
> Stop it?

> ### ROSE
> Amos, there were women...children down there. I knew some of 'em.
> (*Her voice breaks*)
> They were killin' babies.

> ### DRUCKER
> Oh, my God....

Rose leans her head on his shoulder; weeps.

EXT. CHEYENNE CAMP. NIGHT.

Hawk, Crazy Buffalo and the others in the hunting party are tending to the wounds, giving water and doing whatever they can for the few survivors of the massacre, most of whom are elderly men and women, plus a few young children.

After wrapping an Old Woman in a buffalo robe, a distraught, angry Hawk looks about the camp. The sadness in his eyes turns to anger.

Crazy Buffalo, Tall Elk and Yellow Moccasin approach Hawk.

                    CRAZY BUFFALO
          Does Soars Like a Hawk still wish to be a friend to the
          white man, or will he be a Cheyenne?

                    HAWK
          I am a Cheyenne. A Cheyenne warrior chief...and this
          murder of our people will not go unpunished.
                    (*Beat*)
          Ride to the camps of our brother Cheyenne. Tell them to
          meet us in council...so that we can plan our revenge on the
          white dogs who did this.

                                        SMASH CUT TO:

AN ARROW

It flies through the air toward its target.

TROOPER JONES

He is drinking coffee from a tin cup. The only illumination is from a CAMPFIRE.

A THUD, as the arrow hits its target.

A look of surprise crosses Trooper Jones' face. He opens his mouth and blood spills from it. He looks down at his midsection to see the point and shaft of the arrow protruding from it.

EXT. CAMPSITE. NIGHT.

Trooper Jones and a dozen of his fellow Troopers (all in their 20s) who were at Sand Creek have been sitting around a campfire, eating the evening meal. The other Troopers are momentarily stunned, as Jones' corpse pitches forward onto the ground.

                    ANOTHER TROOPER
          Oh, Jesus Christ!

Cheyenne WAR CRIES from the darkness surrounding them.

GUNSHOTS.

Two other Troopers are hit; go down. The remaining Troopers are disoriented.

They grab their weapons; FIRE wildly.

Suddenly, several Cheyenne braves, including Hawk, Crazy Buffalo, Tall Elk and Yellow Moccasin, burst out of the darkness; attack the Troopers with knives.

Most of the Troopers try to flee.

HAWK

With a vengeance, he buries his knife into the gut of one Trooper, then withdraws the weapon; grabs another Trooper from behind and cuts his throat.

CRAZY BUFFALO

He chases down a fleeing Trooper; tackles him, cuts his throat, then takes his scalp. He stands; gives a Cheyenne cry of victory.

YELLOW MOCCASIN

He leaps at a Trooper who has been able to get onto his horse. The two men go sprawling onto the ground with the Cheyenne winding up on top. A crazed look in his eyes, Yellow Moccasin plunges his knife into the Trooper's chest, again and again and again...long after the man is dead.

ANOTHER TROOPER

He has been able to get to his horse and is attempting to get away.

HAWK

He spots the man, grabs one of the trooper's rifles, takes aim and FIRES.

ANOTHER TROOPER

The man falls from the horse, dead.

BACK TO SCENE

The battle has ended. Hawk and the other Cheyenne survey the bloody scene. All of the Troopers are dead. No Cheyenne have been hurt.

SMASH CUT TO:

EXT. RANCH HOUSE. NIGHT.

A ranch house is engulfed in flames. Its Owner lies dead in front of it. Hawk and his band of Cheyenne warriors drive off the livestock.

SMASH CUT TO:

EXT. THE PRAIRIE. DAY.

A Paymaster's wagon, with a guard of perhaps two dozen troopers accompanying it, rolls across the plains.

DRUCKER

He is riding with the troopers.

HAWK

Followed by Crazy Buffalo and the rest of his guerrilla band, he rides to the top of a hill that overlooks the caravan. He gestures that they should attack.

BACK TO SCENE

The Cheyenne attack. The Troopers take cover in nearby brush.

DRUCKER

He FIRES his revolver at the attacking Cheyenne.

BACK TO SCENE

The Cheyenne set fire to the brush.

CRAZY BUFFALO

He FIRES his rifle at the troopers with a mad vengeance.

HAWK

He FIRES his Henry rife at the Troopers.

DRUCKER

He's hit; falls dead.

HAWK

He sees Drucker fall; is momentarily saddened by it. Then, he starts firing again at the Troopers.

BACK TO SCENE

As the Cheyenne swarm over them, the Troopers are defeated.

DISSOLVE TO:

EXT. MOUNTAIN TRAIL. DAY.

A steep mountain trail through a dense wooded area.

LT. ADAM HALL (25), a U.S. Army Cavalry officer in a brand new Eastern-style uniform, maneuvers his horse up the difficult trail.

A West Point graduate from New England, Hall has fought with honor in the War Between the States, but is totally inexperienced about the frontier and its problems. He is also "haunted" by his war experiences, hiding his fears behind a straight-laced, by-the-book demeanor. He reaches a plateau, wipes his brow with a handkerchief, then sees:

ROSE'S CABIN

A small, one-room log cabin, seemingly deserted.

BACK TO SCENE

Hall starts riding toward the cabin. Suddenly, a Figure leaps out of a tree behind him; knocks him off his horse onto the ground. Hall and his attacker go sprawling.

As the Lieutenant starts to turn over onto his back, his Attacker leaps on top of him; presses the blade of a Bowie knife at his throat. Startled, frightened, Hall looks up and sees:

ROSE

There is a crazed look in her eyes. At first, it appears as if she's about to slice his throat open, then she relaxes slightly, as a look of recognition takes over.

>   ROSE
>   You're Army.

BACK TO SCENE

>   HALL
>   Yeah...Lieutenant Adam Hall...at your service.

Rose lowers the knife; gets up.

>   ROSE
>   Sorry 'bout that. Didn't recognize yer uniform. Thought
>   you were one of them Militia bastards.

The Lieutenant is somewhat taken aback by her language.

>   HALL
>   Militia...?

He gets up; brushes himself off.

>   ROSE
>   Yeah. One of the drunks, drifters and thieves that rode with
>   Chivington. Some of 'em aren't too happy with what I had
>   to say to your General Parks.
>   (*Beat*)
>   What the hell you doin' up here anyway?

>   HALL
>   Rose Carmichael?

>   ROSE
>   That's me.

>   HALL
>   General Parks wants to see you.

>   ROSE
>   I don't work for the Army no more.

                    HALL
My orders are to bring you back.

                    ROSE
              (*Brandishes the knife*)
What if I say, "I ain't going"? Your pretty uniform there
could get mussed.

                    HALL
Miss Carmichael, we need your help. The Cheyenne....
They're killing every white man in the territory.

                    ROSE
Can you blame them? After what Chivington did?

                    HALL
General Parks needs a scout with your experience to help....

                    ROSE
                 (*Interrupts*)
Get Amos Drucker. He's the best man you got.

                    HALL
Amos Drucker is dead.

Rose is startled. She'd allow herself to cry, but she's not about to
show weakness in front of Hall.

                    ROSE
Amos is dead?

                    HALL
Last week. The Cheyenne attacked a Paymaster's wagon.
Drucker was with the troops escorting it.
                 (*Beat*)
He was a friend?

ROSE
(*Nods; beat*)
I'll get my horse.

EXT. MOUNTAIN TRAIL. DAY.

It's a few minutes later. Hall and Rose ride back down the trail, retracing the Lieutenant's earlier path.

HALL
(*Hesitantly*)
The General tells me your mother was Cheyenne.

ROSE
You got a problem with that?

HALL
No, I....I just wonder how you can work for the Army...fight the Indians...when you're half Cheyenne.

ROSE
(*Interrupts*)
I'm half Irish, too.

HALL
(*Doesn't see her point*)
Oh.

ROSE
(*Beat*)
Boy, you're really a dumb son-of-a-bitch, ain't you?

Rose boots her horse; rides down the trail ahead of Hall.

EXT. KIRBYTOWN. DAY.

A handbill, offering $2000.00 reward for Soars Like a Hawk, has been posted on a bulletin board outside the saloon. Cochran, Pugh and Bedford emerge from the saloon.

133

COCHRAN
(*Angry; calls back into saloon*)
You're a bastard, Kirby... not extendin' credit to three honest members of the Colorado Militia.

PUGH
(*Parrots him; shouts*)
Bastard!

COCHRAN
(*Sees handbill*)
Would you look at this. They're offerin' a two thousand dollar reward fer that murderin' redskin.

BEDFORD
Could use that two thousand dollars.

COCHRAN
Back in County Cork, they were only offerin' twenty quid fer me....What kind of world is it that values a bloody Injun over a fine strappin' Irishman?

Cochran glances toward the street, and sees:

COCHRAN'S P.O.V.

Hall and Rose enter the town; ride through.

BACK TO SCENE

COCHRAN
(*Indicating Rose*)
Well, look who's back.

BEDFORD
(*Mutters*)
Bitch.

Rose and Hall head out of town, toward:

EXT. ARMY CAMP. DAY.

Establishing shot. An encampment of tents for a well equipped U.S. Army regiment, as they prepare to go out to fight the Cheyenne.

INT. GENERAL PARK'S TENT. DAY.

GENERAL LAWRENCE C. PARKS (55) is tall, bearded; a responsible, fair-minded career officer. Coat unbuttoned, he sits behind his desk, reviewing some documents; smoking a cigar. There are two chairs opposite him. Hall enters and salutes.

> HALL
> I've got the Carmichael woman, sir.

> PARKS
> Bring 'er in.

Hall motions outside the tent to Rose. As she enters:

> PARKS (*cont'd*)
> Hello, Rose. Glad you came.

> ROSE
> (*Non-committal*)
> Humph.

> PARKS
> I'm sorry about Amos. He was a good man. He often told me that he thought of you as a daughter.

> ROSE
> What do you want me for, General?

He indicates that she should sit, which she does. Hall remains standing.

> PARKS
> You've met Lieutenant Hall here....

ROSE
Yeah, I know the dumb son-of-a-bitch.

Hall flushes.

PARKS
I'm glad you're getting along so well.

Rose shrugs.

PARKS (*cont'd*)
(*Beat*)
Rose, while you've been off in the mountains, a Cheyenne warrior chief named Soars Like a Hawk and his band have been raiding ranches, killing dozens of whites.

ROSE
Hawk!?! Used to know that asshole.

PARKS
I beg your pardon?

ROSE
We didn't get along too well.

PARKS
Oh.
(*Beat*)
We've posted a reward for him.

ROSE
Why don't you just give 'im Chivington?

PARKS
What?

ROSE
Give 'em Chivington and he'll stop...probably.

PARKS

If it was that simple, I'd shoot Chivington myself. The bastard starts the biggest Indian war this country's ever seen, then he runs off to California.

HALL

My men and I were fighting in Georgia when the War Department sent us out here.

PARKS

Rose, with Amos gone, you're the best scout in the territory. I need you to help end this bloodshed.

ROSE

I can track 'em for you, General. Then, what?

PARKS

I want to talk to this Hawk. Convince him to join Chief Black Kettle on the reservation.

ROSE

Sure you don't want to just kill 'em all?

PARKS

There's been enough killing...on both sides.

ROSE
(*Gets up*)
All right. Let me tend to some business, then we'll go....Which way's the latrine?

Parks points off in a direction. Rose exits.

PARKS
(*To Hall*)
You look tired, Lieutenant. Maybe the War Department should've let you rest awhile before they sent you out here.

                         HALL
I'm fine, sir...but....

                         PARKS
But, what?

                         HALL
Sir, are you sure we can trust this...woman?

                         PARKS
Yes, lieutenant, I'm sure.

EXT. KIRBYTOWN. DAY.

Cochran, Pugh and Bedford are still loitering around the outside of
the saloon.

Hall and Rose, leading about twenty troopers on horseback, ride
through the town, heading out toward the prairie. Among the group
are SGT. BATES (35), burly, a career soldier, and CORPORAL
DIGGS, 28, tall and slender, also a career soldier.

                         COCHRAN
Billy, me lad, go back into Kirby's and get some of the
boys.

                         BEDFORD
What's up?

                         COCHRAN
I think I got us way to collect that two thousand dollars.

As Bedford re-enters the saloon, Cochran continues to watch the
military unit depart.

                                   SMASH CUT TO:

INT. COVERED WAGON. DAY.

Crazy Buffalo, his face covered with war paint and with the look of the kill in his eye, tears back the cloth covering of the wagon; looks inside.

O.S. a WOMAN SCREAMS.

CRAZY BUFFALO'S P.O.V.

MRS. MAGUIRE, 20s, a frightened white woman, huddles on the floor of the wagon, trying to protect her BABY with her body. She has blond hair.

BACK TO SCENE

Crazy Buffalo boosts himself into the wagon.

EXT. PRAIRIE. DAY.

The Cheyenne, all in war paint, have ambushed three covered wagons, two of which are now in flames. The bodies of several White Men lie on the ground.

Hawk is the leader of the band. As Tall Elk, Yellow Moccasin and three other Cheyenne pick at the dead, he rides over to the wagon that is not burning; looks inside.

HAWK'S P.O.V.

Crazy Buffalo is attempting to force himself onto Mrs. Maguire.

INT. COVERED WAGON. DAY.

Hawk leaps into the wagon; grabs Crazy Buffalo and tosses him outside onto the ground.

EXT. PRAIRIE. DAY.

Hawk jumps down from the wagon; stands over Crazy Buffalo, who reaches for his knife, then thinks better of it.

CRAZY BUFFALO
Soars Like a Hawk forgets that he is Cheyenne...and that she is a white woman.

The other Cheyenne stop what they are doing; move closer.

HAWK
I do not forget....We do not make war on women.

CRAZY BUFFALO
At Sand Creek, the whites made war on our women...and children.

HAWK
We are not the whites.
(*To the other Cheyenne*)
Take the horses. We go.

Disgruntled, Crazy Buffalo picks himself up; goes with the other Cheyenne to collect the team horses. Hawk looks back into the wagon.

HAWK'S P.O.V.

Mrs. Maguire, still very frightened, huddles on the floor of the wagon, protecting her baby.

HAWK

He looks at the blond-haired woman. Perhaps there is something familiar about her; something that evokes a memory.

Then, he walks off to joins his fellow Cheyenne.

WIPE TO:

EXT. PRAIRIE. DAY.

Looking for a trail, Rose rides several yards ahead of Lieutenant Hall and the rest of the troop. She glances up and sees:

ROSE'S P.O.V.

SMOKE rising from just over the next hill.

BACK TO SCENE

> ROSE
> (*Calls*)
>
> Lieutenant!

She points toward the smoke. The Lieutenant sees it. Rose and the soldiers ride at a gallop in that direction.

EXT. THE WAGONS. DAY.

The scene is about the same as we last saw it, except that not much is left of the two burning wagons and the team horses are gone. Rose, followed by Hall and the Troopers, ride up to the wagons. She, revolver in hand, rides over to the still standing wagon; looks inside.

ROSE'S P.O.V.

Mrs. Maguire, still huddled on the floor, holding her baby, gasps when she sees Rose.

BACK TO SCENE

> ROSE
>
> M'am, no need to be scared. We're here to help.
> (*Calls*)
>
> Lieutenant!

As Hall rides over to the wagon, some of the soldiers dismount; check the bodies for any signs of life.

> ROSE (*cont'd*)
> (*To Hall*)
>
> Got a survivor, here.

She rides off. Hall looks inside the wagon.

HALL
You all right, ma'm?

ROSE

She rides around the perimeter of the wagons, looking for a trail.

HALL (*O.S.*)
Sergeant, have a man help this lady and her baby.

SGT. BATES (*O.S.*)
Yes, sir.

BACK TO SCENE

Hall rides over to Rose; points.

HALL
There're signs of horses over there, heading East.

ROSE
That's a false trail. A couple of bucks with the team horses.
(*Indicating the ground in
front of her*)
The main group went this way.

HALL
I don't see anything there.

ROSE
That's why I'm the scout and you're...

She thinks better of calling him a "dumb son-of-a-bitch" in front of his men.

ROSE (*cont'd*)
...the lieutenant.

HALL
(*Irked*)
I believe my eyes, Miss Carmichael.
(*Points to the other trail*)
We're heading East.

ROSE
Not if you want to catch the Cheyenne that did this.

Hall's uncertainty is apparent, but he can't lose face in front of this crass woman whom he distrusts and despises.

ROSE (*cont'd*)
(*Giving him a way out*)
Tell you what. You're gonna be stuck here for a couple of hours or so, burying them fellas...lookin' after the lady and her baby.... Why don't I take a few men...head up this way for a look see?

HALL
(*Beat*)
That sounds reasonable.

ROSE
Good. If I don't find nuthin', I'll be back. Wouldn't want to miss supper.

Hall scowls at her, as she rides back toward the soldiers.

EXT. FOOTHILLS. DAY.

Rose, accompanied by Sgt. Bates and five Troopers, head toward a canyon into the mountains.

BATES
The lieutenant's all right, Rose. He's just got to get educated about what it's like on the frontier, that's all.

ROSE

Well, I ain't no school marm. Hell, I can barely read and write myself.

She spots something on the ground.

ROSE (cont'd)

Let's hold up here.

She dismounts; checks the ground in front of her.

ROSE (cont'd)
(Hands Bates the reins to her horse)

You boys wait here. I'm goin' up aways and have me a look.

Taking her rifle, Rose walks up the trail toward the canyon.

TROOPER

Sarge, what's she tryin' to prove? That she's better than a man?

BATES

Son, out here, she is better than most men.

EXT. CANYON. DAY.

Rose enters the canyon, keeping close to the wall; her rifle ready. She moves slowly forward.

EXT. FUTHER INTO THE CANYON. DAY.

Rose rounds a corner of the canyon and sees:

ROSE'S P.O.V.

A Cheyenne SENTRY sits atop a rock, a rifle across his lap. He is eating his afternoon meal; not paying too much attention to his sentry duties.

BACK TO SCENE

Rose takes a step or two backward. She gets an idea, then retraces her steps back down the canyon.

EXT. FUTHER INTO THE CANYON. DAY.

It's a few minutes later. The Cheyenne Sentry finishes his meal. He stands; looks about, then turns toward the canyon wall and urinates against it. As he finishes, he turns around and sees:

SENTRY'S P.O.V.

Rose stands directly behind him, her rifle butt raised.

ROSE
Howdy!

She smashes the weapon into the Cheyenne's face.

BACK TO SCENE

The Sentry falls backwards onto the ground, unconscious. Rose gives a wave back toward the canyon entrance. Bates and the other Troopers, their rifles ready, round the corner on foot; head toward her.

EXT. HAWK'S CAMP. DAY.

Located in a hidden part of the canyon, with high boulders surrounding it and limited access, the camp is a natural fortress. Hawk, Crazy Buffalo, Tall Elk, Yellow Moccasin and two other Cheyenne sit in a circle, eating their afternoon meal. Hawk and Crazy Buffalo are engaged in a heated discussion.

CRAZY BUFFALO
After Sand Creek, Soars Like a Hawk swore revenge on the whites. Has he forgotten that?

HAWK

I swore revenge on the white dogs who killed our people.
Not women. Not children.

CRAZY BUFFALO

The white man must be sent a message.

HAWK

What message? That we are savages? They already
believe that. We are not savages. We are a people....

Suddenly Hawk's attention goes beyond Crazy Buffalo. His mouth
remains open in astonishment, as he sees:

HAWK'S P.O.V.

Rose has entered the camp, walking behind the Cheyenne Sentry,
who is gagged and whose hands are tied behind his back with
buckskin.

She carries her rifle. She and the Cheyenne stop several yards away
from the group. Her stance is quite masculine.

BACK TO SCENE

Hawk stands; still at a loss for words. Curious, the other Cheyenne
turn in Rose's direction. Their expressions are ones of shock and
disbelief.

ROSE

Hello, Hawk.

HAWK
(*Steps forward*)
I am Soars Like a Hawk.
(*Starts to recognize her*)
You are....

ROSE

Rose Carmichael. General Parks sent me.

HAWK

No, you are Rozene.

ROSE

Was Rozene. Now, I'm Rose.

HAWK

I remember you.
(*Beat*)
You are a woman!?!

ROSE

Yep, I am. Didn't you know that?

CRAZY BUFFALO

She is the mongrel woman.

ROSE

Crazy Buffalo. You're the mean son-of-a-bitch that threw rocks at me.

HAWK
(*Beat*)
The blue coat general sent you?

ROSE

Me and some friends.

She indicates the rocks surrounding the camp.

Hawk looks up/about and sees:

HAWK'S P.O.V.

Sgt. Bates and the other Troopers are situated atop the rocks, each one aiming a rifle at one of the Cheyenne.

ROSE (*O.S.*)

There's a rifle pointed at every one of you.

147

BACK TO SCENE

Hawk and the other Cheyenne realize that they are trapped.

                    ROSE
        Don't fret none. This is a friendly visit.

                    HAWK
                    (*Beat*)
        Why you not dress like woman?

                    ROSE
        Wouldn't know how to....General Parks wants to talk with
        you.

                    HAWK
        Then he should send man. To send woman is an insult.

                    ROSE
        Well, just pretend I'm a man. Everybody else does.

Despite himself, Hawk is intrigued by this woman.

                    HAWK
                    (*Beat*)
        Tell your general that when the last white who was at Sand
        Creek is dead, then we will talk.

                    ROSE
        I was at Sand Creek. You going to kill me, too?

                    HAWK
        You were at Sand Creek?

                    ROSE
        I tried to stop it. Got hit on the head. When I came to, it
        was over.

CRAZY BUFFALO
She lies!

Hawk stares at Rose long and hard, then:

HAWK
She not lie.
>(*Beat; to Rose*)

You are part Cheyenne. Why do you ride with the whites who did this?

ROSE
The whites I ride with were not at Sand Creek.
>(*Beat*)

The leaders back in Washington are ashamed at what happened at Sand Creek. They want to make it up to the Cheyenne.

HAWK
>(*Sarcastic*)

How would they do that? Will they bring back Crazy Buffalo's sister... my bride-to-be?

ROSE
You were promised to Little Butterfly?

Hawk nods.

HAWK
Will the leaders in Washington punish the men responsible?

ROSE
The son-of-a-bitch governor...the asshole who appointed Chivington... has been booted out, and Colonel Chivington ....Hell, he's run off to California someplace. They don't know where exactly he is.

HAWK

They are alive, and the women and children of Sand Creek are dead.

ROSE

Yeah, they're alive.

HAWK

Then, how will they make "make it up" to the Cheyenne?

ROSE

Chief Black Kettle is goin' to move his tribe to a reservation in the Oklahoma Territory. The Government'll give them cattle, teach 'em how to grow their own food....

HAWK

They will be fed like dogs.

CRAZY BUFFALO

The Cheyenne eat their dogs.

ROSE

The white man's war in the East will be ending soon. Many blue coats...
(*Indicates Bates and the Troopers*)
...like the ones up there...but with greater weapons... will be coming West. If Soars Like a Hawk and his brothers fight them, they will be destroyed.

HAWK

Many blue coats will also die.

ROSE

General Parks will grant you and your brothers amnesty...if you will lay down your weapons and join Black Kettle on the reservation.

HAWK

Generals lie.

ROSE

This one speaks the truth.
(*Beat*)
Besides, he said that after you talk to him, if you can't come
to terms, he'll give you a six hour head start before he sends
the troops out after you again.

HAWK

The General promise that?

ROSE
(*Poker-faced*)

Yeah.

SGT. BATES AND TROOPER

They stand next to each other on the rocks above the Cheyenne
camp, their rifles pointed at the Indians.

TROOPER

Sarge, can she say that?

BATES

Whatever works, son.

EXT. CANYON. DAY.

Rose and Hawk, followed by Crazy Buffalo, Tall Elk, Yellow
Moccasin and the rest of the Cheyenne ride through the canyon,
heading out toward the prairie. Sgt. Bates and the Troopers ride
behind them. The Cheyenne still have their weapons.

CRAZY BUFFALO
(*Indicating Rose*)

The mongrel woman is not to be trusted. She is leading us
into a trap.

ROSE

It's no trap.

HAWK

I will hear the white General's words...look into his
eyes...then I will decide.

CRAZY BUFFALO

Soars Like a Hawk has still not decided if his heart is with
the whites or the Cheyenne.

Angry, Crazy Buffalo turns his horse; re-joins the rest of the
Cheyenne behind Hawk and Rose.

ROSE

Still an angry fella, ain't he?

HAWK

If Crazy Buffalo misses a buffalo with his arrow, he gets
angry at the buffalo. That's why he is called Crazy Buffalo.

As the group continues through the canyon and starts up an incline,
Sgt. Bates rides up to Rose.

BATES

Rose, I'm thinkin' that I should ride on ahead. Alert the
Lieutenant that these Injuns are comin' in peaceable.

ROSE

Good idea.

Bates starts to ride on ahead of the group, when:

An O.S. GUNSHOT.

Bates is hit in the chest; falls off his horse, dead.

More O.S. GUNSHOTS.

Yellow Moccasin is hit, killed.

Two other Cheyenne braves are also killed. One of them falls from
his horse, tumbles down the embankment.

COCHRAN & COMPANY

Cochran, Bedford, Pugh, Frank, Bart and two other reprobates, who we will call TOM and DICK (both in their 20s), are positioned at various spots atop the canyon, FIRING their rifles down at the Cheyenne and the Troopers. There is no escape from their gunfire.

HAWK

His horse is hit by a bullet. It rears up, then stumbles. Hawk is thrown, smashing into Rose, who is beside him. The force knocks both of them off of their mounts and they tumble down the embankment.

BACK TO SCENE

More O.S. GUNSHOTS.

Tall Elk is killed.

BOTTOM OF HILL

Rose and Hawk recover from their tumble down the steep embankment. He realizes that he only has a knife. She only has her revolver.

> HAWK
> (*Brandishing his knife at her*)
> You led us into an ambush!

> ROSE
> (*Points revolver at him*)
> You crazy? They're shootin' at me, too.

Realizing that she makes sense, Hawk lowers the knife.

COCHRAN AND BEDFORD

Situated atop the canyon, they continue to shoot at the Cheyenne.

BEDFORD
Which one is Soars Like a Hawk?

COCHRAN
Damned if I know....Aim for the troopers.

He FIRES several rounds at the soldiers, as does Bedford.

THE TROOPERS

Two soldiers are hit; go down. The other Troopers are in a state of confusion. They FIRE their weapons wildly toward the top of the canyon.

One Trooper, not sure who is shooting at him, SHOOTS one of the Cheyenne in the back, then is struck down by a bullet from above.

BOTTOM OF HILL

Hawk starts back up the hill.

HAWK
They are killing my brothers.

ROSE
Hey! What're you gonna fight 'em with?

Hawk stops.

BACK TO SCENE

Crazy Buffalo, rifle in hand, has jumped off his horse and taken cover behind a rock. BULLETS RICOCHET off the rock, as he takes aim with the rifle; FIRES.

TOM

He's hit; comes tumbling down the hill, dead.

COCHRAN AND BEDFORD

> BEDFORD
> That son-of-a-bitch!

As Cochran draws a bead on Crazy Buffalo:

> COCHRAN
> Don't be frettin' about ol' Tom there.

He FIRES his rifle.

CRAZY BUFFALO

He's hit in the forehead; falls dead.

COCHRAN AND BEDFORD

> COCHRAN
> (*Lowering his rifle*)
> That's one less split of the reward money.

BOTTOM OF HILL

Rose and Hawk see Tom's body reach the bottom of the hill.

> HAWK
> You know him?

> ROSE
> Seen 'im in town. He hangs around the saloon.

More O.S. GUNFIRE.

A dead Trooper comes tumbling down the embankment.

> ROSE (*cont'd*)
> Christ, it's a damn massacre....They don't want no
> witnesses.

Hawk takes a revolver from Tom's corpse; starts back up the embankment. Rose grabs his arm.

ROSE (*cont'd*)
You can't fight 'em with that. They got rifles. The high ground.

HAWK
I will not abandon my brothers.

ROSE
They're dead.
(*Beat*)
Now, let's get the hell outta here before those bastards come after us....We'll get back at them later.

Seeing the wisdom of Rose's words, Hawk nods; heads into some underbrush. Rose follows.

BACK TO SCENE

Apparently all of the Cheyenne and Troopers are dead, as Cochran, Bedford and the rest of the group of ambushers make their way down from the top of the canyon. Their rifles are at the ready.

COCHRAN
Look for the Injun with the Henry. That'll be Soarin' Hawk or whatever his bloody name is.

Bedford and the others start checking the bodies.

As Cochran surveys the corpses, he sees:

COCHRAN'S P.O.V.

A wounded Trooper, moves, moans.

BACK TO SCENE

Cochran, casually, SHOOTS the Trooper in the back of the head.

COCHRAN
(*Calls*)
And make sure they're all dead.

Bedford, looking over the bodies, sees:

THE HENRY

The rifle lies next to Hawk's dead horse, which is right next to the edge of the embankment.

BACK TO SCENE

BEDFORD
(*Brandishing the Henry*)
Here's the Henry.
(*Indicates embankment*)
Figure the Injun fell down there.

Cochran takes the Henry from Bedford.

COCHRAN
Take one of the boys an' go down an' check. He ain't worth nuthin' to us down there, is he?

Bedford motions to Dick, and the two men, both with rifles, start down the embankment.

BEDFORD
(*Turns back to Cochran*)
I don't see the Carmichael bitch. Maybe she's down there, too.

COCHRAN
(*Taunting*)
Well, Billy Ray, she's the one I'd be watchin' out for.

Bedford scowls at Cochran, then heads down the embankment with Dick.

COCHRAN (*cont'd*)
(*To his other men*)
Boys, let's move these bodies around a bit. Make it look like a fight between the Injuns and the troopers 'stead of an ambush.

He looks admiringly at the Henry rifle.

BOTTOM OF HILL

Bedford and Dick reach the bottom of the embankment; look about for bodies.

BEDFORD
Damn!

He surveys the ground for tracks.

BEDFORD (*cont'd*)
(*Points toward underbrush*)
Looks like they went that way.
(*Calls up the embankment*)
Jimmy!

Cochran appears at the top of the embankment.

COCHRAN
(*Calls*)
You find 'em?

BEDFORD
They're runnin'. South, I think.

COCHRAN
Start after 'em. We'll go around. Try to head 'em off.

BEDFORD
(*Bitter*)
Great!

Bedford and Dick head into the underbrush.

BACK TO SCENE

COCHRAN
(*To Bart*)
Get their horses. Give 'em a hand.

Bart nods; heads for the horses.

EXT. RAVINE. DAY.

Rose and Hawk emerge from the underbrush into a ravine that leads away from the canyon. As they hurry along the ravine:

ROSE
Hold up!

Hawk stops, as she drops; puts her ear to the ground and listens.

ROSE (*cont'd*)
(*Getting up*)
There's two of 'em comin'...on foot.

Hawk gets down onto the ground and listens. As he gets up:

HAWK
(*Impressed with her ability*)
Who teach you this?

ROSE
Amos Drucker.

HAWK
Drucker?

ROSE
He raised me after my Pa died....Are you the one that killed him?

> HAWK
> (*Shakes head*)
I did not seek Drucker's death.

> ROSE
Well, wherever he is, I'm sure he's happy to know that.

> HAWK
> (*Beat; indicates underbrush*)
These men. We stop them here.

> ROSE
Damn right, we stop 'em here. If they got rifles, I don't
want to be out in front of 'em.

EXT. UNDERBRUSH. DAY.

Their rifles ready, Bedford and Dick hurry through the tall grass and
tumbleweeds. Bedford pauses for a moment to catch his breath, as
Dick moves forward.

EXT. RAVINE. DAY.

As Dick emerges from the underbrush, his rifle at the ready, he sees:

DICK'S P.O.V.

Rose is standing a few yards down the ravine; hands on her hips,
looking at him.

BACK TO SCENE

> DICK
> (*Calls over his shoulder*)
Billy Ray!

EXT. UNDERBRUSH. DAY.

Bedford hears Dick's voice; moves forward.

EXT. RAVINE. DAY.

As Dick raises his rifle to shoot Rose, Hawk suddenly leaps out from behind a rock, grabs him around the neck with one arm; knifes him in the back with his free hand.

BLOOD SPURTS out of Dick's mouth. He collapses to the ground, dead.

Hawk takes the dead man's rifle. Rose starts walking back to join the Cheyenne.

BEDFORD

He emerges from the underbrush, rifle ready, and sees:

BEDFORD'S P.O.V.

Hawk's back is turned toward him, but Rose is looking directly at him.

BACK TO SCENE

Rose sees Bedford; draws her revolver.

ROSE
Bedford, you goddamn son-of-abitch!

She FIRES a wild shot that just misses him.

Hawk turns toward Bedford, rifle in hand.

Bedford blanches; FIRES a shot toward Rose, which goes wild. Then, he turns tail and rushes back into the underbrush.

Rose rushes toward the underbrush, FIRING her revolver.

ROSE (cont'd)
Come back here, you bastard!

EXT. UNDERBRUSH. DAY.

With GUNSHOTS being fired behind him, Bedford rushes back along the path he came. He stumbles once; picks himself up and continues on.

EXT. RAVINE. DAY.

Rose reaches the underbrush and is about to pursue Bedford, when:

> HAWK
>> Rozene!

Rose stops; looks at him.

> HAWK (*cont'd*)
>> Do not follow him in there.

> ROSE
>> (*Beat*)
>> You're right...but the name is Rose.

> HAWK
>> Rose.

> ROSE
>> (*Beat*)
>> That Bedford....He's always hangin' around with Jimmy Cochran...an' Cochran was one of the top dogs in Chivington's militia.

> HAWK
>> Why they kill the soldiers?

> ROSE
>> They gotta be after the bounty.... Your scalp is worth a lot of money, Hawk.

> HAWK
>> I think I keep it for awhile.

ROSE
Then, let's get the hell outta here.

They head down the ravine.

WIPE TO:

EXT. CANYON. DUSK.

Lt. Hall, Corporal Diggs and about a half-dozen Troopers enter the canyon, trying to re-trace the trail left earlier by Rose, Sgt. Bates and the others. As they round a bend, Hall reins his horse when he sees:

HALL'S P.O.V.

Corpses of Bates, the Troopers and Cheyenne are on the ground, arranged to look as if they were fighting each other.

HALL (O.S.)
Oh, my God!

BACK TO SCENE

Hall, Diggs and the Troopers are shocked...angered.

HALL
(To Diggs)
See if there's anyone alive here.

DIGGS
Yes, sir.

He dismounts; starts checking the bodies. Hall, still on horseback, moves slowly through the scene.

HALL
I don't see the Carmichael woman. Do you?

WIPE TO:

EXT. FOREST CLEARING. DUSK.

A heavily wooded area with a trail leading through to a small clearing.

Cochran, Bedford, Pugh, Bart and Frank ride into the clearing; rein their horses. The men look about.

> BEDFORD
> They couldn't've gotten this far. They're on foot.

> COCHRAN
> Billy Ray, you bloody fool. You should've kept after 'em.

> BEDFORD
> They were shootin' at me.

> COCHRAN
> Too bad they didn't hit ya.
> *(Beat)*
> Let's backtrack. Spread out.

The men turn their horses around; head back the way they came.

HAWK AND ROSE

They have been hiding behind some rocks and bushes. After the ambushers disappear from sight:

> ROSE
> Okay, let's get goin'.

She starts off.

> HAWK
> Where you go?

> ROSE
> I'm gonna try an' meet up with the Army, so they can go after Cochran and those bastards....Coming?

                    HAWK
Maybe I go after Cochran and those bastards myself.

                    ROSE
    Are you stupid?

Her remark surprises Hawk. Nobody has ever dared call him
"stupid" before.

                ROSE (*cont'd*)
                (*In his face*)
    The general's offerin' you amnesty, and you're goin' out and
    start killin' again?

                    HAWK
    I must avenge my brothers.

                    ROSE
    The Army'll take care of Cochran. They killed soldiers,
    too.
                    (*Beat*)
    Christ, Hawk, I knew you were an asshole, but I didn't think
    you were a dumb son-of-a-bitch, too.

Has Hawk even heard this word before?

                    HAWK
    Asshole?

                    ROSE
    Yeah, asshole.

She starts off again.

                ROSE (cont'd)
                (*Over her shoulder*)
    Come on. Let's go find someplace to hole up fer the night.

Hawk hesitates a moment, then follows.

> HAWK
> (*To himself*)
Asshole.

They move off into the trees.

INT. CAVE. NIGHT.

A small cave, hidden behind some trees. Rose and Hawk sit by a small fire, eating some jerky. They eat in silence for a several moments, as Hawk studies Rose, then:

> ROSE
What?

> HAWK
Why you live with whites...and not Cheyenne?

> ROSE
'Cause the whites treat me better than the Cheyenne.

> HAWK
Cheyenne not treat you good?

> ROSE
Hell, no! Crazy Buffalo, Yellow Moccasin...other braves...kicked me...threw rocks at me when I was little...just 'cause my Pa was white.

> HAWK
I did not throw rocks at you.

> ROSE
You didn't stop them.
> (*Beat*)
You called me "mongrel".

HAWK
(*Matter-of-fact*)
You half-breed. You mongrel.
(*Beat*)
I remember, you cry like white child...not Cheyenne.

ROSE
I don't cry no more....Asshole!

HAWK
(*Snaps*)
No more "Asshole"!
(*Beat*)
You half-breed. How whites treat you better?

ROSE
They treat me better 'cause they need me. I'm the best scout
in the territory.

HAWK
They treat you better because you talk like man...fight like
man... dress like man?

ROSE
Damn right.

HAWK
How good they treat you if you dress like woman?

ROSE
(*Beat*)
Go to Hell!

She scrambles to her feet; stomps out of the cave.

EXT. PRAIRIE. DAWN.

A temporary camp for Lt. Hall and his Troopers, set down in a
shallow ravine that affords cover. There is one Sentry.

Hall and Corporal Diggs are conferring over a map. The other Troopers are dowsing a campfire; gathering up their bedrolls, as they get ready to pull out.

EXT. FOREST. DAWN

Hawk and Rose crouch down at the edge of the forest, watching the Troopers, who are about three hundred yards away.

> ROSE
> I'll go in. Tell the lieutenant what happened. Then, I'll signal you.

> HAWK
> Good.

Rose gets up; walks out onto the prairie, heading toward the Army camp. Hawk keeps low; watches.

EXT. PRAIRIE. DAWN.

Hall and Corporal Diggs are still conferring over the map, when Diggs glances up; sees something.

> DIGGS
> (*Points*)
> Lieutenant....

Hall turns around and sees:

HALL'S P.O.V.

Rose is walking across the prairie, heading into the camp.

BACK TO SCENE

> HALL
> (*Waves Diggs into action*)
> Corporal....

Diggs grabs his rifle. He signals Two Troopers to follow him with their rifles at the ready, then the three soldiers double time out of the camp to meet up with Rose.

HAWK

Crouched low, he watches from the forest.

ROSE

She sees Diggs and the Troopers approaching her.

> ROSE
> (*Waves; friendly*)
> Hiya, boys!

The three soldiers reach her. The Troopers grab hold of each of her arms.

> ROSE (*cont'd*)
> What the...!

Diggs relieves her of her revolver.

> ROSE (*cont'd*)
> What's goin' on here?

> DIGGS
> Lieutenant wants to see ya.

As they start escorting her toward the camp:

> ROSE
> Get yer goddamn hands off me!

She struggles, but the Troopers hold her tight.

HAWK

He moves back into the forest.

BACK TO SCENE

Diggs and the Troopers enter the camp; bring Rose to Lieutenant Hall.

>   ROSE
> Hall, you stupid bastard, what the hell is goin' on here?

>   HALL
> Keep your mouth shut, woman....You are under arrest for treason and murder.

Rose can't believe what she is hearing.

>   HALL (*cont'd*)
> You will be taken back to the fort...tried under military law and, most likely, hung.

>   ROSE
> Are you crazy!?!...I didn't pull off the ambush.

>   HALL
> What ambush?....I saw the bodies, woman....Yours was the only one not there.
>   (*Beat*)
> I told the general he shouldn't trust a half-breed.

>   ROSE
> It's Miss Half-Breed to you, you son-of-a-bitch!

Rose suddenly pulls out of the grasp of the two troopers; hauls back and punches Hall square in the face. He goes sprawling. The Troopers grab her again; force her arms behind her back.

Diggs suppresses a smile.

Hall, his nose bloodied, would like to shoot Rose right on the spot. He grasps his sidearm in its holster, then relaxes the grip.

HALL
We'll add striking an officer to the charges. That's also a
hanging offense.
(To Diggs)
Tie up the prisoner. Gag her. Let's break camp.

Holding his nose, he walks off.

ROSE
(As she's led off.)
Damn it to Hell, let go of me!

COCHRAN'S P.O.V.

The scene VIEWED AT A DISTANCE THROUGH A SPYGLASS.

COCHRAN (O.S.)
They got 'er all right.

EXT. MESA. DAWN.

Cochran, Bedford, Pugh, Bart and Frank are crouched low on a
mesa, located about a mile away from the soldier's camp. Cochran
watches the camp through a spyglass.

COCHRAN
They're tying her up and gaggin' her...which means they
don't believe her.

He gets up; goes to his horse.

COCHRAN (cont'd)
Bart, get down there and put a bullet in the bitch before
they do.

BART
Why me?

COCHRAN
'Cause you're the best shot among us.

He takes the Henry from his saddle holster; tosses it to Bart.

> COCHRAN (*cont'd*)
> Here! Take the Henry...but bring it back.

Bart mounts his horse; starts down the mesa.

> COCHRAN (*cont'd*)
> (*Calls*)
> Don't let 'em see you.

EXT. PRAIRIE. DAY.

Lt. Hall and his company have started to move out, riding along the edge of the ravine. Rose's hands are tied to the back of a pack horse, thus she is walking. One Trooper rides behind her.

BART

He rides into the ravine about a hundred yards behind the soldiers; dismounts and, carrying the Henry, moves along the arroyo, looking to get a good shot at Rose.

BACK TO SCENE

The military unit, with Rose on foot, continues along its way, unaware of Bart's presence.

BART

He finds a good vantage point; leans against the side of the ravine and takes aim with the Henry.

ROSE

Walking along the ravine, she is in the Henry's sight.

BART

He adjusts his aim; starts to squeeze the trigger.

HAWK *(O.S.)*

My rifle.

Bart looks around and sees:

BART'S P.O.V.

Hawk is standing behind him, holding the rifle he took from Dick. He smashes Bart in the face with the butt.

HAWK

He retrieves the Henry from the unconscious Bart, then carrying both weapons, heads down the arroyo toward Bart's horse.

BACK TO SCENE

Hall and his men ride single file along the prairie.

ROSE

She is having a rough time keeping up with the horse that she's tied behind. At one point, she stumbles, falls and is dragged a few feet. She is able to pull herself to her feet; continue.

REAR GUARD TROOPER

He smirks; amused by her difficulties. After a few moments, he senses something behind him. He turns around and sees:

TROOPER'S P.O.V.

Hawk, on Bart's horse, has ridden up behind him. He swings the butt of the Henry at him.

ROSE

Hearing a THUD, she turns and sees:

HAWK

He grabs the reins of the Trooper's riderless horse.

ROSE

Her eyes express her happiness to see him.

BACK TO SCENE

Hall and the other Troopers are unaware of what is going on behind them.

HAWK AND ROSE

He cuts her hands free. She removes her gag; jumps onto the Trooper's horse, who gives out with a LOUD WHINNY.

DIGGS

The Corporal glances around and sees:

DIGG'S P.O.V.

Hawk and Rose are about to ride off.

BACK TO SCENE

                              DIGGS
                             (*Calls*)
          Lieutenant!

He pulls his rifle from his saddle holster; takes aim.

HAWK AND ROSE

They start to ride off, heading for the forest.

O.S. GUNSHOT.

Rose is hit in the back of the shoulder. Her horse rears up.

BACK TO SCENE

Lt. Hall and the other Troopers come about.

HAWK AND ROSE

She stays on her mount. Hawk grabs the reins of her horse and the pair gallop off toward the forest.

COCHRAN'S P.O.V.

The scene VIEWED AT A DISTANCE THROUGH A SPYGLASS.

COCHRAN (*O.S.*)
Damn that Bart!

EXT. MESA. DAY.

Cochran, Bedford, Pugh and Frank watch Hall and the Troopers start after Rose and Hawk.

COCHRAN
If they get into those woods, they'll never find 'em...and neither will we.

FRANK
We could circle around. Pick 'em up on the other side.

COCHRAN
One thing's fer sure. We can't let 'em be talkin' to nobody.

EXT. PRAIRIE. DAY.

Hawk and Rose are riding fast toward the forest, increasing the distance between them and the pursuing soldiers, who are FIRING at them. Rose is bleeding; in pain, yet she stays her horse. Hawk and Rose reach the forest; disappear in among the trees.

HALL AND COMPANY

As the Lieutenant and his men reach the edge of the forest, Hall raises his hand, signaling the Troopers to halt.

> DIGGS
> What's the matter, sir?

> HALL
> I once led a unit into a wooded area like this....There was a Confederate sharpshooter in every tree....Only three of us got out alive.

> DIGGS
> Sir, they're getting away.

> HALL
> Then, we'd better go after 'em.
> (*Beat*)
> Corporal, send a man back to the fort. Tell the General we need reinforcements.

> DIGGS
> (*Beat*)
> Yes, sir.

Hall leads the company into the forest.

EXT. FOREST CLEARING. DAY.

As Hawk and Rose ride into the clearing, a groggy Rose falls from her horse onto the ground. Hawk dismounts goes to her.

> ROSE
> (*Struggling to get to her feet*)
> Get outta here. They'll catch you.

> HAWK
> Come, we must go.

As he helps her to her horse:

> ROSE
> Hawk...why'd you come back for me?

> HAWK
> Maybe...because...I not stop them from throwing rocks at you.

He lifts her onto her horse, then slaps the other horse, sending it off along the trail. He leads the horse, with Rose riding it, off the trail into the density of the woods toward a large rock formation.

A clump of brush and weeds hides a narrow passage between the rocks. As Hawk leads the horse into the passage:

HALL AND COMPANY

They ride into the clearing, then follow the trail that the riderless horse took into the woods.

EXT. ROCK FORMATION. DAY.

Hawk helps Rose off of the horse; lies her onto the ground. She is doing all she can to keep from losing consciousness.

> HAWK
> We wait here.

> ROSE
> Leave me, Hawk. I ain't gonna make it.

> HAWK
> Maybe Rozene should stop trying to be man and start acting like woman.

> ROSE
> What's that supposed to mean?...An' the name's Rose.

HAWK

Mean...not talk so much.

ROSE

You afraid of women who talk back?

HAWK

I knew woman like you. Talked back. Would not listen.

ROSE

Little Butterfly?

HAWK

No. White woman.

ROSE

A white woman!?!

HAWK

She very confusing.

ROSE

But, you liked her.

HAWK

I had feelings for her.

ROSE

What happened?

HAWK

Our worlds were different. She go to Oregon.

ROSE

Maybe you like women who talk back.

HAWK

I like woman who knows she's woman.

Rose ponders that.

EXT. EDGE OF FOREST. NIGHT.

Hawk and Rose emerge from the forest. He is leading the horse with her riding it. His Henry ready, Hawk looks about, but sees nothing, except:

HAWK'S P.O.V.

A small ranch house and barn are about two miles in the distance.

BACK TO SCENE

Hawk leads the horse toward the ranch.

EXT. HANSON RANCH. NIGHT.

A small ranch house, a barn, corral, well and privy, surrounded by some trees; stuck out in the middle of nowhere. A few horses are in the corral; some cattle grazing nearby. A vegetable garden and very small cornfield are near the house. About a hundred yards from the ranch yard is a shallow gully.

There is a light on in the house, as Hawk, quietly, leads the horse, with Rose riding, into the ranch yard, heading for the barn. She is sweating profusely.

The barn door CREAKS slightly, as Hawk opens it; leads the horse inside.

INT. BARN. NIGHT.

Hawk leaves the door slightly ajar to let in the light. He helps Rose off of the horse; lays her gently onto a bed of hay; feels her head.

                         HAWK
          You very hot.

ROSE
Got a fever.

He sees a horse trough; goes to it and fills a nearby bucket with water. He brings the bucket back to Rose; splashes water onto her face.

EXT. HANSON RANCH. NIGHT.

ANNA HANSON (22) comes out of the house, carrying a bucket. She is an attractive, dark-haired Swedish immigrant, wearing a plain dress and apron. She goes to the well. As she fills the bucket, she glances up and sees:

ANNA'S P.O.V.

The barn door is partly open.

BACK TO SCENE

Anna leaves the bucket at the well; goes to the barn to close the door.

INT. BARN. NIGHT.

Anna takes a step inside to make sure everything is okay, sees:

ANNA'S P.O.V.

Hawk is kneeling beside Rose, helping her drink some water.

BACK TO SCENE

Startled, Anna emits a involuntary scream.

INT. RANCH HOUSE. NIGHT.

It's a one-room structure; a fireplace with cut wood and an axe beside it, a double bed; simple handmade furniture with a few small items that betray the fact that the occupants are originally from Sweden.

Oskar Hanson, Anna's husband, has been reading his Bible. He hears the scream.

INT. BARN. NIGHT.

Anna is frozen to her spot. Hawk stares at her for a moment, then:

> HAWK
> I will not hurt you.

Anna doesn't move.

> HAWK (*cont'd*)
> (*Indicating Rose*)
> My friend is hurt.

He takes a step toward her.

> HAWK (*cont'd*)
> We take food...water...go.

Their eyes meet. Though she is frightened, Anna believes him.

> ANNA
> How is he hurt?

> HAWK
> Bullet. I think it go all way through. But, fever.

> ANNA
> In Sweden, I was nurse assistant at hospital.

Hawk is grateful for Anna's offer. He stands aside for her. She goes to Rose; kneels beside her.

> ANNA (*cont'd*)
> She is a woman!

> ROSE
> Wish people would stop tellin' me that.

As Hawk moves closer to Anna.

> ANNA
> She has fever. We must take her to the house.

O.S SOUND of RIFLE BEING COCKED.

Hawk and Anna turn to see:

HANSON

He stands in the doorway of the barn, holding a rifle pointed at Hawk.

> HANSON
> You get away from my Anna.

BACK TO SCENE

> ANNA
> Oskar, no! This woman is hurt.

> HANSON
> (*Indicating Hawk*)
> He's...He's an Indian.

> HAWK
> (*His hands raised*)
> I will not hurt you.

> HANSON
> They are the ones the Army lieutenant told us about.

> ANNA
> (*To Hanson*)
> Help carry her into the house.

> ROSE
> Damn it! I can walk.

She tries to get up, but collapses.

> ANNA
>
> Oskar!

Hanson, with some hesitation, lays down his rifle; goes to Rose and picks her up. As Hanson carries her past Hawk and out of the barn:

> ROSE
>
> Hey, Hawk....
> > (*Indicating Anna*)
> She talks back, too.

Hawk suppresses a smile, as he follows Hanson and Anna out of the barn.

INT. RANCH HOUSE. NIGHT.

Her clothing removed, Rose lies in the bed, covered with a blanket. Her injured shoulder is bandaged.

Anna approaches, carrying a small bowl; sits on the edge of the bed.

> ANNA
> Here, this broth will help break your fever.

Rose allows Anna to feed her the broth with a spoon.

> ANNA (*cont'd*)
> That Indian...Hawk...he cares for you.

> ROSE
> Naw, I'm just another one of his braves.

> ANNA
>
> He cares for you.

She feeds Rose another spoonful of broth.

EXT. RANCH HOUSE. NIGHT.

Hanson is sitting on the porch in a chair. Hawk sits on the porch step. Each man, wary of the other, has his rifle close at hand. Hawk drinks from a bowl.

HAWK

This good broth.

HANSON

My wife is a good cook.

HAWK

You say that soldiers were here?

HANSON

This afternoon. They said that you and the woman had killed several of their company.

HAWK

That lie. White men ambush us. Kill soldiers...my brothers.

HANSON

White men?

HAWK

Same white men who were at Sand Creek.

Hanson blanches at the mention of Sand Creek. He looks at his rifle, but does not reach for it.

HAWK (*cont'd*)
(*Noting his reaction*)

You were at Sand Creek?

He glances at the Henry; considers picking it up.

184

HANSON
(*His eyes grow moist with shame*)
I didn't hurt anybody. I never even fired my gun.

HAWK
Then why you there?

HANSON
Indians have been stealing our horses...some cattle....I don't
know what Indians...just Indians....Men came to our ranch,
said they were going to get our horses back...that I should
come with them to help.
(*Beat*)
All I wanted was my horses back.... I didn't know what
those men would do....That they would kill....
(*Beat*)
It made me sick.

Hawk studies Hanson for a long moment, then:

HAWK
A good man does not follow his evil brothers.
(*He drinks more broth*)
Your wife is good cook.

DISSOLVE TO:

EXT. RANCH HOUSE. DAWN.

Hanson and Hawk have slept on the porch, each covered by a
blanket. Hanson is in the chair. Hawk leans against one of the
support posts. Their rifles are next to them.

ROOSTER CROWS O.S.

As the men awaken, the door opens and Anna comes out.

HAWK
(*Stands*)
How is she?

ANNA
Better. Her fever broke. She's weak, but she wants to get up.... She's a stubborn woman.

Hawk nods in agreement.

HANSON
I better feed the livestock.

He starts for the barn.

HAWK
(*Follows him*)
I help.

EXT. PRAIRIE. DAWN.

Cochran, Bedford, Pugh, Frank and Bart (his face bruised from being hit by Hawk) rein their horses.

COCHRAN
Billy, me boy, who ever gave you the idea that you could follow a trail?

BEDFORD
You did.

COCHRAN
Well, I was mistaken.
(*Takes a drink of water from his canteen, then:*)
I think we better change our strategy.

BEDFORD
How that?

COCHRAN
Split up. Each one of us go in a different direction. See what we can find.

                    BEDFORD
    And, then?

                    COCHRAN
    If one of us finds the two of 'em, follow 'em. Just leave a
    trail that the rest of us can follow.

                    PUGH
    How'll we know if one of us finds 'em if they don't come
    back and tell us?

                    COCHRAN
    Good question, Brian. You're thinkin'.
                    (*Beat*)
    Them of us that don't find 'em will meet back here at, say,
    noon. If somebody don't show up, then the rest of us'll just
    head out in his direction and look for his trail.

EXT. RANCH YARD. DAY.

Hawk and Hanson finish feeding the horses in the corral.

                    HANSON
    How 'bout some breakfast.

                    HAWK
    Good.

As the men walk back toward the house, the door opens.

HAWK

He looks up and sees:

HAWK'S P.O.V.

Rose emerges from the house, wearing a plain gingham dress. Her
arm is in a make-shift sling and she is not too steady on her feet, but
she looks beautiful. Anna steps out behind her.

HAWK

His mouth drops.

BACK TO SCENE

                    ROSE
              (*Notes Hawk's reaction*)
        What?

Hawk is momentarily speechless.

                    ROSE (*cont'd*)
        All right. I'm in a dress. She cut my other clothes off.

                    HAWK
        Rozene is very handsome woman.

                    HANSON
        She is.

                    ROSE
                  (*Blushes*)
        Stop it!

                    HAWK
              (*Smiles, chuckles*)
        Very handsome.

                    ROSE
              (*Brandishes fist*)
        Damn it, Hawk. You laugh at me and I'll smack you right in
        the face.

                    HAWK
        I not laugh...I....

He nods his approval.

Frustrated, unsure, Rose doesn't know how she should react to Hawk. She looks at Anna.

> ANNA
>
> You are.

Rose knows that, if she doesn't get out of there, she's going to burst into tears and she won't allow Hawk to see that side of herself. She hurries back into the house, leaving Hawk slightly bewildered.

INT. RANCH HOUSE. DAY.

Hanson and Hawk sit at the table, eating pancakes, as Anna and Rose serve them. Rose, though feeling somewhat awkward doing domestic chores, does seem to enjoy it. Hawk has trouble keeping his eyes off her, but every time Rose glances in his direction, he looks away.

> HANSON
>
> What are you going to do now, Hawk?

> HAWK
>
> Maybe go North. Join my cousins, the Sioux.

> HANSON
>
> More killing?

> HAWK
>
> That for white man to decide.
> (*Beat*)
> I, one time, believe that the Cheyenne is like a mountain lion. He is wise. He does not attack a stronger foe like the grizzly bear. He avoids him....Now, I not so sure.

> ANNA
>
> Rose, what about you?

> ROSE
>
> I don't know. I'm finished here. That's for sure. If I stay, the Army'll probably hang me.

HAWK

Come with me....I will not let them throw rocks at you.

ROSE

Thanks, Hawk...but my life is in the white world....I just gotta find a new place to live it.

EXT. RANCH YARD. DAY.

Bedford rides into the empty ranch yard; glances around.

INT. RANCH HOUSE. DAY.

Having heard the rider outside, everyone tenses. Hawk reaches for his Henry. Hanson goes to the window, moves the curtain back slightly; looks outside.

HANSON

I know him.

EXT. RANCH YARD. DAY.

Seeing nobody about, he rides over to the house.

BEDFORD
(*Calls*)

Anybody home?

Hanson, carrying his rifle, steps outside.

BEDFORD (*cont'd*)

Hiya.

HANSON

Good morning.

BEDFORD

Hey...weren't you with us at Sand Creek?

Hanson doesn't respond.

BEDFORD (*cont'd*)
That was a helluva day, wasn't it?

HANSON
(*Beat*)
What do you want?

BEDFORD
My friends and me are part of a posse, looking for a
murderin' redskin and a renegade half-breed bitch that
ambushed an Army column....You ain't seen 'em, have you?

HANSON
I've seen them.

BEDFORD
Yeah? Which way did they...

He stops mid-sentence, as Hawk and Rose emerge from the door
behind Hanson.

Hawk has the Henry pointed at Bedford.

Rose takes a revolver out of her sling; aims it at the ambusher. They
stand on either side of Hanson, while Anna stands in the doorway
behind them.

BEDFORD (*cont'd*)
...go?

ROSE
The truth is, Oskar, that Bedford here is one of the
murderin' sons-of- bitches that ambushed them soldiers.
An', he wants Hawk an' me dead, so's we don't tell no one.

BEDFORD
Oskar, you gonna take that half-breed's word over mine...a
white man.

Hanson doesn't answer, but the expression on his face, says
"Absolutely".

> HAWK
>
> Get off horse.

> BEDFORD
>
> You go to hell, Injun.

He turns his horse, attempting to get away. Hawk steps forward and,
using the Henry as a club, swings the weapon, hitting Bedford across
the back of the head.

Bedford falls off the horse onto the ground.

> BEDFORD (*cont'd*)
> (*Shakes his head;*
> *turns over on his back*)
>
> Shit....

Standing over Bedford, Hawk cocks a shell into the chamber of the
Henry; gets ready to shoot him.

> HANSON
>
> Hawk, don't!

> HAWK
>
> He kill my brothers. He should die.

> HANSON
>
> Let the Army do it. If you turn him over, he can prove that
> you and Rose weren't part of the ambush.

> ROSE
>
> He's right, Hawk.

> HAWK
>
> Will Army hang white man for killing Cheyenne?

HANSON
They will for killing soldiers.

ROSE
Dead is dead, Hawk.

Hawk lowers the Henry.

ROSE (*cont'd*)
(*Walks over to Bedford*)
Where's Jimmy Cochran and the rest of your bunch?

BEDFORD
Around. When I don't come back, they'll start lookin' for me...an' when they find me, they're gonna burn this place out.

ROSE
Well, maybe we'll surprise 'em.

She exchanges glances with both Hawk and Hanson, both of whom nod agreement.

BEDFORD
(To Hanson)
You sure you want to be throwin' in with these two, Oskar?

ROSE
Shut up, asshole!

She gives him a swift kick in the face, knocking him out.

ROSE (*cont'd*)
(*To Hawk and Hanson*)
We said, don't shoot 'im. Nobody said nuthin' 'bout kicking him.

INT. RANCH HOUSE. DAY.

Hawk, Hanson and Rose are getting their respective guns ready for the upcoming fight with Cochran's men. Anna is preparing coffee and a meal. Bedford, his face bruised and bloodied, is tied to one of the house's support posts. After a few moments, Hawk stops what he is doing; looks at the Hansons.

                    HAWK
          This is not your fight.

                    ANNA
          It's our land. Our fight.
                    (*Offers a mug*)
          Coffee?

EXT. PRAIRIE. DAY.

Cochran, Pugh, Frank and Bart ride toward the Hanson ranch, following Bedford's trail. A few hundred yards away, they rein their horses. Cochran peers through his spyglass and sees:

COCHRAN'S P.O.V.

Anna is doing her washing; hanging clothing and sheets onto the clothesline.

BACK TO SCENE

                    COCHRAN
          Well, what do we have here?

                    PUGH
          It's a ranch.

                    COCHRAN
          Thank you, Brian.

He continues to look over the ranch, and he sees:

COCHRAN'S P.O.V.

The corral, which among other horses, holds Bedford's mount.

BACK TO SCENE

> COCHRAN
> Billy Ray's here alright.

> PUGH
> How do you know?

> COCHRAN
> That's his Bay in the corral.

> PUGH
> Where is he?

> COCHRAN
> Probably inside the house....Looks like he found himself some female company.

He kicks his horse, leading the group toward the ranch yard.

EXT. RANCH YARD. DAY.

As Cochran and company head toward the ranch, Anna is definitely aware of their presence, but she does not let on.

INT. RANCH HOUSE. DAY.

Bedford is on the floor, hands tied behind his back, a gag in his mouth.

Hanson is by the window, rifle in hand.

EXT. RANCH YARD. DAY.

The barn door is slightly ajar.

INT. BARN. DAY.

Still in the dress, Rose watches from a slightly ajar barn door. She has discarded her sling, and is wearing her gunbelt; holds a rifle at the ready.

EXT. PRAIRIE. DAY.

As they near the ranch yard, Cochran looks about. A sixth sense tells him that something is not quite right.

> COCHRAN
> (*To Pugh and Bart*)
> You boys hang back a bit. Frank, let's go in an' have a look see.

Cochran and Frank ride into the ranch yard.

EXT. RANCH YARD. DAY.

Anna is briefly disturbed that Cochran and Frank have come into the yard alone. She momentarily rests her hand on the butt of a revolver that is hidden beneath her apron; hides her concern with a welcoming smile.

> ANNA
> Good morning, sir.

> COCHRAN
> 'Morning to you, ma'm. And how are you on this fine day?

> ANNA
> Just fine.

THE GULLY

Hawk, rifle ready, lies on his stomach, waiting for the right moment to make his move.

Unfortunately, Bart and Pugh are positioned just in front and above him, so that he is unable to get off a shot without first revealing his position.

BACK TO SCENE

ANNA
(*Indicating well*)
Would you and your friends like to fill your canteens?

COCHRAN
That's very kind of you, ma'm. Thank you.

ANNA
(*Indicating Bart and Pugh*)
Have your friends come in.

COCHRAN
Actually, ma'm, I wanted to ask you about that Bay in yer corral there. Looks like one that belongs to a mate o' mine.

ANNA
Oh, do you know Mr. Bedford?

COCHRAN
Billy Ray and me are like brothers.

ANNA
He's inside eating his breakfast.

INT. RANCH HOUSE. DAY.

With Hanson's attention elsewhere, Bedford is trying to work his tied hands free, rubbing them against a nail in the wall.

ANNA (*O.S.*)
(*Continuing*)
Would you like to join him?

EXT. RANCH YARD. DAY.

Cochran considers Anna's offer for a moment, then:

COCHRAN
Why don't you ask him to step out here?

ANNA

She reaches down and, again touches the revolver hidden beneath her apron.

COCHRAN

He notes her move, and:

BACK TO SCENE

In one swift move, Cochran draws, cocks and points his revolver directly at Anna's chest.

COCHRAN
Don't make me shoot you, ma'm. It'd be such a waste.

INT. RANCH HOUSE. DAY.

Hanson blanches at the sight of his wife in danger.

HANSON
(*To himself*)
Anna....

EXT. RANCH YARD. DAY.

COCHRAN
(*Calls toward house*)
Billy Ray! Get your bloody ass out here!
(*To Anna*)
Beggin' yer pardon, ma'm.

THE GULLY

Though he can't see the ranch yard from his position, Hawk knows that something is wrong and that he must make a move. He jumps to his feet; aims his rifle.

BART

He spots Hawk.

BART
(*Shouts*)
It's an ambush!

COCHRAN AND FRANK

They turn their attention toward Bart.

HAWK

He FIRES his rifle.

BART

He's hit in the chest; falls dead.

PUGH

He spots Hawk; draws and FIRES his pistol at him.

HAWK

The shot misses him.

ROSE

She steps out of the barn; raises her rifle and FIRES.

FRANK

He's hit in the back of the head; falls off his horse, dead.

The frightened animal bolts; gallops out of the ranch yard.

COCHRAN

He FIRES two shots in Rose's direction.

ROSE

Still holding the rifle, she dives behind the corral, out of sight.

HAWK

He FIRES at Pugh; misses.

INT. RANCH HOUSE. DAY.

Hanson FIRES his rifle through the window.

EXT. RANCH YARD. DAY.

The bullet strikes the side of the well; ricochets harmlessly away.

Anna draws her revolver; FIRES it at Cochran. She misses. Cochran's horse rears up, but he controls it.

> COCHRAN
> (*To Anna; indicating Hawk*)
> 'Scuse me, ma'm. He's the one I want.

He rides toward Hawk; FIRING his pistol as he goes.

COCHRAN AND PUGH

They both ride toward Hawk, FIRING their pistols.

HAWK

He dives for cover back into the gully.

INT. RANCH HOUSE. DAY.

His hands now untied, Bedford rushes Hanson; grabs the rifle and hits him across the face with the butt, knocking him to the ground.

BEDFORD
(*Pointing the rifle at him*)
I oughta kill you right now, you son-of-a-bitch!

Instead, he turns his attention to the front door.

EXT. THE GULLY. DAY.

Hawk races down the ravine, with Cochran and Pugh chasing him on horseback.

EXT. RANCH YARD. DAY.

Rose, on her feet, sees that Cochran and Pugh are pursuing Hawk. She starts after them on foot.

EXT. THE GULLY. DAY.

Cochran and Pugh are almost upon Hawk when the Cheyenne suddenly spins; FIRES his rifle.

PUGH

He's hit point blank; falls off his horse, dead.

COCHRAN

He momentarily reacts to his companion's demise.

HAWK

He seizes the opportunity to rush up the side of the gully; leap up at Cochran and knock him off his horse. The two men go sprawling.

HAWK AND COCHRAN

The two men struggle. Hawk, knife in his hand and hate in his eyes, is out for blood. Cochran was, after all, the leader of the ambush.

EXT. RANCH YARD. DAY.

Bedford emerges from the house, rifle in hand, and, without her being aware of him, hurries up behind Anna. Bedford grabs Anna from behind; wrestles her to the ground and disarms her.

HAWK AND COCHRAN

As the Cheyenne is getting the best of the Irishman and is about to plunge the knife into his chest:

TWO SHOTS O.S.

Hawk looks up and sees:

HAWK'S P.O.V.

In the ranch yard, Bedford is holding Anna. One arm is wrapped around her neck and the other is holding a six-gun to her temple.

> BEDFORD
> (*Shouts*)
> Give it up, Injun!

HAWK

He's torn. He wants to kill Cochran more than anything, but Anna is being threatened. He raises his arm, ready to finish Cochran, then suddenly drops his hand to his side; a sign of surrender.

ROSE

She reaches the gully; climbs down into it.

HAWK AND COCHRAN

Cochran gets to his feet; glowers silently at Hawk, looks down at Pugh's corpse, then back at the Cheyenne.

HAWK
(*He wants to kill him*)

You no hurt those people.

COCHRAN
(*Picking up his hat and revolver*)

I don't give a bloody damn about them.
(*Points revolver at Hawk*)
You and Rose in there are the ones I want....Now, tell 'er to get her ass out here.

Hawk looks straight at Cochran. His eyes convey his nonverbal response, "No".

Cochran points his revolver straight at Hawk's forehead.

COCHRAN (*cont'd*)

Do it!

Hawk doesn't budge. Cochran pulls back the hammer of the revolver.

COCHRAN (*cont'd*)

Now!

Seeing that Hawk is not going to obey:

COCHRAN (*cont'd*)
(*Lowers the revolver*)

To hell with it.

Suddenly, he smashes Hawk across the face with the weapon, knocking him down onto the ground. He points the gun at Hawk's head.

COCHRAN (*cont'd*)
Guess I'll just have to get 'er myself.

He is about to shoot, when:

ROSE (*O.S.*)
Jimmy!

Cochran turns and sees:

COCHRAN'S P.O.V.

Rose is standing below him in the gully, her rifle pointed directly at him.

ROSE
Drop the goddamn gun.

BACK TO SCENE

His revolver still pointed at Hawk, Cochran hesitates, not sure whether he should follow Rose's command or try to shoot her. As he weighs his chances:

ROSE (*cont'd*)
You're right. To hell with it.

She FIRES the rifle, hitting Cochran square in the forehead. A stunned expression on his face, he falls dead.

Rose scrambles up the gully; rushes over to Hawk.

ROSE
Are you all right?

She embraces him. He holds her close.

HAWK
I all right.

ROSE
(*Suddenly embarrassed by her feelings,*
she pushes away)
I'd've been here a lot sooner if it weren't for this goddamn dress.

They turn their attention toward the ranch yard.

BEDFORD

Realizing he is alone, he panics; FIRES a wild shot in Hawk's direction.

ANNA

She breaks away from him; heads for the house.

BEDFORD

He FIRES another wild shot at Hawk; turns and starts to run, trying to catch Anna.

HAWK

He grabs Cochran's revolver; jumps onto his horse and gallops toward Bedford.

BACK TO SCENE

Bedford catches up with Anna, just as she reaches the front porch. He grabs hold of the back of her dress; pulls her backward down onto the ground.

HAWK

He bears down on Bedford; FIRES several shots at him.

ROSE

Her rifle in hand, she hurries after Hawk on foot.

BACK TO SCENE

Bedford is about to pull Anna up from the ground and use her as a shield.

HANSON

He comes barreling out of the house, brandishing the axe.

> HANSON
> (*Shouts*)
> You leave my Anna alone!

BEDFORD

He turns toward Hanson, just as:

HANSON

He swings the axe.

BEDFORD

The axe blade is buried deep into his chest. Blood spurts from both the wound and Bedford's mouth.

ANNA

She gasps.

BEDFORD

He falls dead.

HAWK

He reins his horse just inside the ranch yard, as:

BACK TO SCENE

Hanson rushes over to Anna. They embrace.

ROSE

She stops just outside the ranch yard. She watches the couple.

HAWK

He looks back at Rose.

ROSE

She looks at Hawk.

BACK TO SCENE

Hawk and Rose stare at each other for a long moment, pondering their situation.

DISSOLVE TO:

EXT. RANCH YARD. DAY.

Hawk stands by his horse, saying his good-byes to the Hansons.

HAWK
You good people. I wish you well.

HANSON
You're still heading North?

Hawk nods.

HANSON (*cont'd*)
When the Army asks, we'll tell them that you went South.

Hawk nods his appreciation; gets onto his horse.

Rose comes out of the house, wearing clothes that she's borrowed from Hanson. They're a bit big for her, but she's making them work.

She heads for the corral where another horse is saddled.

HANSON (*cont'd*)
Rose...?

ANNA
Rose, we should ride back to the fort with you. Tell the officers what happened here.

ROSE
Not goin' back to the fort. But, you can tell 'em anyway...so they won't be lookin' for me.

HAWK

He watches her, wondering...hoping.

BACK TO SCENE

ANNA
Where will you go?

ROSE
(*Gets on her horse*)
Don't know for sure.
(*Beat*)
Never seen California....And, I ain't been up North for awhile.
(*Beat; to Hawk*)
You want some company?

Hawk's non-verbal response says, "Sure".

ROSE (*cont'd*)
I figure if I don't like it up there, I can always try California.

She smiles with affection at Hawk. He returns the smile.

DISSOLVE TO:

EXT. PRAIRIE. DAY.

Hawk and Rose ride together toward the horizon.

> ROSE
> (*Facetious*)
> Just don't let them Sioux throw rocks at me.

> HAWK
> If they do, I smack them right in the face.

They share a warm laugh together, then continue riding toward the horizon.

FADE OUT.

THE END

AFTERWORD

Now that you've finished reading the two screenplays, it's time to talk about them.

We're starting on a fairly equal footing, since until I began putting this book together; I hadn't looked at either of them for about eight years. You might say that I have approached them with fresh eyes. There were a lot of scenes in both that I'd completely forgotten about.

After a first read through, I definitely preferred my initial script, *Cheyenne Warrior II* over *Hawk*, which is, essentially, a romantic action movie. Like its predecessor, *Cheyenne Warrior II* has a "soul," an epic quality that, in some ways, defines the plight of Native Americans.

As I remarked in the Introduction of this book, had *Cheyenne Warrior II* been filmed and done well, I felt that it could have led into a third and final part of the story, climaxing with Soars Like a Hawk joining up with his Cheyenne and Sioux brothers to defeat General George Armstrong Custer at the Battle of the Little Big Horn, which was the final great victory of the Plains Indians against the United States.

Or, it could have served as a backdoor pilot for a television series that would have been somewhat of a Native American version of "The Fugitive," in which Hawk, the U.S. Army and bounty hunters on his trail, travels around the West, getting involved with different people and their problems each week.

But, all that is a writer's fantasy.

Just before writing this Afterword, I, once again, read both scripts and, I must admit, that I also like *Hawk*, but for a different reason.

211

"Rose Carmichael" was a fun character to write. My inspiration for her was, of course, Calamity Jane, the American frontierswoman and professional Army scout. In fact, like with Rebecca in the original *Cheyenne Warrior*, this second script is really Rose's story, not Hawk's. I didn't intend it to happen, it just turned out that way.

Hawk may not have the epic values of the other screenplay, but it is a pretty good romantic action movie, sort of a Western version of *The African Queen*.

You'll note, by the way, that there is no dialogue within quotation marks in *Hawk*. One note I received from Roger's people when I submitted the first script was that the Cheyenne would speak English. Subtitles in a movie cost money.

It's my understanding that Roger Corman had planned to shoot the sequel in Canada, since the Simi Valley location where *Cheyenne Warrior* was filmed is now filled with houses. However, once the script was completed, the situation in that country to the north had changed. Financial incentives that had drawn movie producers to Canada were no longer available, so both *Cheyenne Warrior II* and *Hawk* were put on the shelf to gather dust.

About a year or so later, Roger offered me the opportunity to direct *Hawk*, providing I could find the locations that would work for a Southern California filming. Apparently, he was negotiating some sort of arrangement with Screen Actors Guild that would make a local shoot financially feasible.

Hawk would not be an inexpensive movie to shoot, due particularly the Sand Creek and a few other major action sequences. However, Roger and I had already discussed avoiding much of that cost by employing the often used practice of purchasing stock footage from a previously shot Western (e.g. *Soldier Blue*, 1970), then seamlessly inserting those shots into our film. Indeed, when I was working on these two scripts, I watched *Soldier Blue*, then wrote the Sand Creek Massacre and other action scenes in such a way that they could easily incorporate the earlier footage.

I spent a week or two running all over Los Angeles and vicinity, scouting locations, everywhere from the caves at Bronson Canyon to the Vasquez Rocks to a couple of studio ranches. I probably shot a half-dozen rolls of film.

Sadly, when I presented my report to Roger, he informed me that the deal he was trying to negotiate with SAG had fallen through.

The script went back onto the shelf and that's where it has stayed.

Luckily, I retained the publishing rights to both screenplays, which is why you are now getting what might be your only opportunity to ever learn what becomes of Soars Like a Hawk.

I hope you enjoyed these scripts and, if so, please let me know which one you liked best.

Michael B. Druxman

ABOUT THE AUTHOR

Michael B. Druxman is a veteran Hollywood screenwriter whose credits include *Cheyenne Warrior* with Kelly Preston; *Dillinger and Capone* starring Martin Sheen and F. Murray Abraham; and *The Doorway* with Roy Scheider, which he also directed.

He is also a prolific playwright, his one-person play, *Jolson*, having had numerous productions around the country. Other produced stage credits include one-person plays about Clark Gable, Carole Lombard, Spencer Tracy and Orson Welles. These and plays about Errol Flynn and Clara Bow have been individually published under the collective title of *The Hollywood Legends*.

Additionally, Mr. Druxman is the author of fifteen other published books, including several nonfiction works about Hollywood, its movies, and the people who make them (e.g., *Basil Rathbone: His Life and His Films*, *Make It Again, Sam: A Survey of Movie Remakes*, *One Good Film Deserves Another: A Survey of Movie Sequels*, *Merv* [Griffin] and *The Musical: From Broadway to Hollywood*).

He has written two novels, *Nobody Drowns in Mineral Lake* and *Shadow Watcher*, a book of short stories, entitled *Dracula Meets Jack the Ripper & Other Revisionist Histories*, plus the humorous revisionist history, *Once Upon a Time in Hollywood: From the Secret Files of Harry Pennypacker*, and *Family Secret*, a non-fiction book co-authored with Warren Hull, which reveals the true facts behind the 1947 murder of mobster "Bugsy" Siegel in Beverly Hills.

An acknowledged Hollywood historian, he has also written television documentaries and has been interviewed for various retrospective featurettes that have accompanied DVD releases of classic films (e.g. *The Maltese Falcon*, etc.).

Mr. Druxman is a former Hollywood publicist of 35 years experience who has represented many film and television stars, as well as noted directors, producers and composers. One of his Academy Award campaigns is often mentioned in books dealing with Oscar's history.

He has taught various dramatic writing and film appreciation courses in an adult university and is the author of *How to Write a Story...Any Story: The Art of Storytelling*, which has been used as a text in several colleges. He is often invited to speak to groups of aspiring film and television professionals to discuss screenwriting and the realities of show business.

A native of Seattle who graduated from Garfield High School and the University of Washington, Mr. Druxman moved with his wife, Sandy, from Los Angeles to Austin, TX in 2009.

His memoir, *My Forty-Five Years in Hollywood and How I Escaped Alive*, is published by Bear Manor Media.

Other Published Screenplays by

Michael B Druxman

Cheyenne Warrior

Ghoul City

Matricide

Sarah Golden Hair

Uncle Louie

All questions with regard to these screenplays should be addressed to the author:

Michael B. Druxman
PMB 119
4301 W. William Cannon Dr.
Suite B-150,
Austin, TX 78749
[*druxy@ix.netcom.com*]